Ten Minute Tales

By

Westcliff-on-Sea Women's Institute
(WoSWI) Writing Group

Foreword by Karen Maitland

Published by WoSWI Writing Group

©Westcliff-on-Sea Women's Institute
(WoSWI) Writing Group 2015

This book is copyright.
Subject to statutory exception and to provisions of relevant collective licensing agreements, no part of this publication may be reproduced without the prior written permission of the author(s).

This is a work of fiction.
The characters, places and events are the product of each author's imagination or are used fictitiously.
Any resemblance to actual persons, living or dead,
is purely coincidental.

Published by WoSWI Writing Group

ISBN 978-0-9934063-0-0

Edited by Kim Kimber
(www.kimkimber.co.uk)

With thanks to
Barbara Bowen BA (Hons)
for her cover drawing of the locket

Proceeds from this anthology are being divided between The South Essex Branch of the Motor Neurone Disease Association (Registered Charity No. 294354) and Westcliff-on-Sea Women's Institute (WoSWI) (Registered Charity No. XT 36711)

Writing prompts from The Writer's Toolbox
reproduced with kind permission of:
Jamie Cat Callan, www.JamieCatCallan.com
and Chronicle Books, 680 Second Street, San Francisco
CA94107

*Celebrating 100 years
of the
Women's Institute*

Contents

Foreword *1*

Introduction *3*

Sources of Inspiration *5*

The Picnic *9*

Bella and the Tattoo *17*

Karma *21*

A Lovely Cup of Tea *29*

The Session *35*

Money for Nothing *39*

Garden Party *45*

The Sins of the Father *51*

Pool Party *57*

Forever Young *65*

Moving Mum *67*

The Locket *75*

Joanie's Locket *77*

Pandora's Box *85*

Lost and Found *89*

Norman's Conker *99*

A Flock of Seagulls *107*

Blue *115*

Millennium Bug *123*

Double Trouble *135*

Saving Mother *139*

The Ripper *145*

Camper Van *153*

Peppers, Paps and Old Pals *159*

Carnage in the Kitchen 165

Bernard! 171

Shake, Rattle and Run 175

Westchurch Surprise 179

The Perfect Day 187

Blue Kite in a Tree 189

The Sea and Southend Pier 191

About the Authors 193

Westcliff-on-Sea Women's Institute 197

The South Essex Branch of the Motor Neurone Disease Association 199

Foreword

I was delighted when, in 2013, Westcliff-on-Sea Women's Institute (WoSWI) chose one of my novels as their big summer read and invited me to speak. But I must confess to being somewhat startled when I arrived to see the speaker's table covered in knitted breasts of all colours. Was this a competition and, as guest speaker, would I be expected to judge them? And what on earth would I award points for – firmness, perkiness, originality?

Then an even worse thought occurred to me – was I in fact the wrong author? Had they spent the summer reading *Fifty Shades of Grey*, and were expecting to be addressed by E.L. James? It had happened to me once before, at the start of my writing career, when I'd been asked to speak at a major writing conference only to realise, to my horror, as I listened to the person introducing me, that they were expecting the novelist, Sara Maitland. Their secretary had invited the *wrong* Maitland. Fortunately for me, the organisers at WoSWI were far more efficient and, no, I did not have to judge any kind of knitting competition.

After the meeting, I had a great time talking with members of the writing group who had recently published their own anthology, *Write on the Coast*. I read a copy on the train going home. It was delicious as a box of handmade chocolates, the stories and poems, all different, but containing luscious and unexpected fillings.

The members of this very talented writing group have now produced this, their second anthology which contains a wonderful assortment of fiction and poetry; *Ten Minute Tales*. In it you will also find their own unique series of interlinked tales, *The Locket,* which reveals the stories of the people who have owned, inherited, lost, found and loved this piece of jewellery over six decades from 1940–2000.

This is the perfect summer read, just the collection to slip into your pocket and dip into on the train, in the garden or on those lazy afternoons on the beach. Half of the royalties from each book will be donated to the Motor Neurone Disease Association, so you know when you buy this book you are helping a really good cause. Enjoy!

Karen Maitland (Novelist)

Introduction

Following the success of our first book, *Write on the Coast*, in 2013, Westcliff-on-Sea Women's Institute (WoSWI) Writing Group is proud to have published a second anthology, *Ten Minute Tales*, with proceeds helping to support a very worthy cause; the South Essex Branch of the Motor Neurone Disease Association.

It is hard to believe that WoSWI Writing Group is now in its fourth year and retains many original members. The group continues to meet on a monthly basis to offer support, encouragement and critique. It is wonderful to see how our ideas, however small, can develop into a story that can inspire, sadden, anger, uplift or give cause for reflection.

In recent months, the group has explored a variety of different ways to generate ideas for stories and these are explained in greater detail at the beginning of each section. We hope that these will be useful to other writing groups and encourage anyone interested in putting pen to paper to have a go.

Shortly after the publication of *Write on the Coast*, WoSWI was lucky enough to have author Karen Maitland come along to one of our meetings to talk about her books, after her historical novel *The Falcons of Fire and Ice* was chosen for our annual summer read. Karen has had a fascinating life and not only turned out to be an engaging speaker but an encouraging mentor who stayed behind to chat to us – even buying a copy of our anthology. During her talk Karen touched on the books she has written in collaboration with other authors and the difficulties and rewards of co-writing. With Karen as our inspiration, the writing group decided to have a go, a venture that proved to be a lot more difficult than we anticipated. *The Locket*, a collection of seven stories covering more than half a century is the result.

Another source of inspiration has been *The Writer's Toolbox* by Jamie Cat Callan, a collection of cleverly designed exercises that provide a framework around which would-be writers can weave their stories. In addition to being a good starting point, the writing prompts also turned out to be great fun and it was interesting to see how differently they were interpreted by members of the group.

Proceeds from *Ten Minute Tales* are being shared between Westcliff-on-Sea Women's Institute (WoSWI) and the South Essex Branch of the Motor Neurone Disease Association and more information about these two organisations can be found at the end of this book.

In her foreword, Karen graciously described our previous anthology as being 'delicious as a box of handmade chocolates', an analogy that we hope will apply equally to *Ten Minute Tales*. Dip in and enjoy!

Kim Kimber
(Editor and founder of WoSWI Writing Group)

Sources of Inspiration

In recent months the writing group has been working with a series of prompts from *The Writer's Toolbox* by Jamie Cat Callan.

What started as a five minute warm-up exercise in the group sessions, quickly turned into an obsession as we took it in turns to choose three sticks at random from the ones in the box, each containing a sentence or clause on which to base our stories.

And what fun we had! From exotic dancers and famous actresses to cheating spouses and wailing children, we created characters that have made us laugh and cry until our sides hurt. We are pleased to be able to share a selection of those stories with you in this anthology.

The sentences are printed at the beginning of each section and are italicised in each story or poem so look out for them; they often give rise to the most unlikely twist and bizarre turn of events.

Michael sat down in the middle of the road and began to cry...

On the following Friday we packed our bags and planned our escape.

The thing she did to the brakes on the Honda.

The Picnic

Josephine Gibson

Michael sat down in the middle of the road and began to cry. The poor little boy had had enough.

"Mummy," he wailed, "Beanie is squashed and he's DEAD now."

We were all feeling stunned and not sure what to do next, or where to direct our attention. Michael's lonely whimpers rose above the scene of the accident like smoke from a fire that had just been extinguished with a bucket of cold water, and the adults were the soaking wet ashes floating directionless. It was Pete who managed to pull himself together first.

"Now don't worry, Michael," he said, "Beanie is a brave old soul and is probably just concussed. We'll get him to hospital and we'll see what the doctors can do. He'll be alright, you'll see."

His reply galvanised us into action and we began to gather things together; the wreck of the ruined picnic, the broken crockery, the scattered chairs and the bent pushchair. With some effort Pete managed to partially collapse the pushchair so that we could fit it into the car, but as I turned round after wiping Michael's nose I noticed him give the car a kick on the bumper. I could understand his frustration.

He and Meg had been under such pressure at work. Both full time teachers in a busy secondary school, they'd been blindsided by a critical OFSTED report that had upset the whole teaching staff and led to management reviews and meetings right in the critical revision period leading to exams. John and I minded the grandchildren while they worked and we were aware of the late hours and extra time they were putting in.

"I wish there was something more we could do to help," I worried at John while he was shaving one morning. "Meg's morning sickness means she's half dead by the time they get home, and poor Pete has to bath the children and do the chores as well as staying up late working half the night."

"Humph!" John exhaled, causing beads of shaving foam to float towards the mirror (I could see I'd have to wipe it when he'd finished). "We already look after their children five days a week, feed them dinner and you do their ironing. And now Meg's pregnant again. Honestly, I ask you, hasn't she got the idea of contraception yet?"

"Oh, John, there's no point going over that again. It's happened and we'll just have to manage."

"Well, it's hardly the retirement I expected," he said, rattling his razor in the water self-righteously.

I ignored him, he was such an old woman sometimes. Worse than me, anyway. And so unkind. He relished the time with Michael after we'd picked him up from school and, although little Susie was still too young to talk, he often said that his grandchildren had given him a second chance, his hard work when Pete was a little boy had paid off now. He'd taken early retirement and was able to spend hours constructing Lego with Michael, his engineering skills as much in evidence with a toy cantilever bridge as it had been building motorways. But it promised to be a long retirement and we had to make our money last, so there was little we could do to help Pete financially...

Ah – unless – a thought struck me and I almost skipped out of the bathroom in my excitement. John had spent his years building motorways, we often joked I had spent my years building a support network amongst the women of my acquaintance. A network that could be utilised in times of crisis, to say nothing of the Easter holidays.

Within a day it was all organised, and *on the following Friday we packed our bags and planned our escape.* A friend of my friend Beverley was selling her holiday cottage and various delays in the process had led to it being vacant and available for a peppercorn rent. "After all," she said, "I can't let it to anyone commercially at this short notice."

So Pete, Meg, Michael, Susie, John and I, together with an assorted menagerie of must-travel toys, including Michael's beloved Beanie and Susie's Panda, set off for a week away in Devon in their trusty Honda people carrier.

Unfortunately, what I had not factored into my plan was the early Easter and the south-west's wet weather. Not only did it rain incessantly but there was a bitterly cold wind. Meg, in the throes of an unexpected early pregnancy, was persuaded to rest as much as possible, leaving Pete, John and I to don waterproofs and wellington boots and to visit a series of tourist attractions along with the thousands of other young families seeking to escape the weather. Personally, I think I managed quite successfully to keep my temper despite the humid hell of being shut in Farmer Fred's Playbarn with a myriad of much worse behaved children than my own, including John who whinged:

"I really think we should have our own holiday...I didn't give up work for this...This should be a holiday for us, without grandkids, being as we look after them all term time...You know, I really think it is time for Meg to give up work..."

"Oh, John dear, I've just remembered I left Susie's drink in the car. Could you be a love and pop out for it? Oh, and I think there are some Werther's Original left in the glove box..."

What a relief when the rain stopped on our last day and a gentle sunshine illuminated the dripping trees and the very lush green grass. A perfect spring day.

"Now," I said, "it's a lovely day for a teddy bears' picnic. Michael, Susie, go and collect Beanie and Panda. John, Pete, we'll need those folding chairs from the outhouse. Meg, dear, do sit down, I've already got it organised."

And indeed I had. I'd already found a beauty spot with the River Dart running through it, a clapper bridge from which to throw Pooh Sticks, a small cafe for cups of tea and the inevitable ice cream, and parking on the road next to the river bank so that Meg could shelter in the car if she felt sick or cold.

Michael's shrieks of delight as he clambered over rocks, calling out to Grandpa and Dad to follow, made the whole effort worthwhile. The picnic was laid out in front of the car, our old tartan blanket surrounded by chairs for the grown-ups, Susie's pushchair ready for her to sit in to eat when she was tired of toddling. Having insisted on driving us here, Meg had elected to stay in the car, ostensibly to keep an eye on the picnic but really, I believed, to have a break from the children.

"Now, Michael," I warned, "be careful climbing on those rocks – Pete, you'd better be ready to catch him!"

"Oh, Mum, stop fussing. He's still small, he's got a low centre of gravity."

And indeed, Michael seemed as agile as a mountain goat as he clambered on the granite boulders that a long-gone torrent must have hurled down the valley. His little face was pink with exertion as he pulled himself up a particularly large one and turned to face us. Even darling Susie gamely tried to follow, sticking a straight leg up against the rock in an attempt to climb.

"Ha ha!" Michael boasted to Pete, "I'm the king of the castle, you're the dirty rascal! Daddy, Daddy, look! What's happened to the car?"

We spun round.

"My God! The brakes must have failed!" Pete shouted and started to run.

John and I grabbed the children and following, saw Meg climb out of the driver's seat and survey the wreckage. The car had rolled forward onto the picnic and come to rest against a boulder. Pete, realising Meg was OK, put an arm round her and then bent down to see if the car was damaged. John, ever practical, leapt into the driver's seat and reversed the car back over the picnic blanket before my shout to stop had reached his ears. Michael, running forward, was the first to realise that Beanie had been directly underneath the front tyre. The little toy, always slightly grubby, was now blackened and, sadly, split along the seam.

In the peace of our bedroom later that afternoon, as the children watched a DVD snuggled up with Meg and Pete, and I was in the process of mending Beanie with my emergency sewing kit, I asked John what he thought had happened. After all, Meg had been sitting in the car. John and Pete had tested the brakes straight away and they were working. Had Meg somehow been at fault?

"Huh!" hissed John "*The thing she did to the brakes on the Honda*! Silly moo, hadn't put the handbrake on! That's what happens with pregnant women, you know, brain all over the place."

"Oh," I said, snipping the thread free of the needle as I finished stitching Beanie, "Well, it's all over now and even Beanie survived. Ooh, pass me that cup of tea, John," and I gestured at it, needle still between thumb and forefinger. "Sorry, dear, I didn't mean to scratch you."

Bella and the Tattoo

Sue Duggans

Spring sunshine streamed through the windows of the cottage. Flowers filled the garden with vibrant colour and heady scent. Michael's beloved Honda 1800 Gold Wing stood freshly-polished by the side wall. The cottage was idyllic and perfectly isolated.

We met and fell in love following a rum-fuelled, passionate, whirlwind romance in Puerto Rico. Michael had been working at the beachside gym in San Juan and his smouldering good looks, amazing physique and dark sparkling eyes had taken my breath away. Michael celebrated our new-found love with a heart-shaped tattoo bearing our initials – 'KM'.

"This for my beautiful Kristie," he told me.

He returned with me to England bringing with him a small holdall, his savings and a visitor's passport. We found the cottage, which I rented, and he stayed illegally. That was nearly two years ago.

Soon after our return I got a job in the restaurant of a local hotel. It paid the bills but meant that I had to work weekends which wasn't ideal. The first crack in our pretty perfect relationship appeared when Michael returned home, cock-a-hoop, having blown most of his savings on a motorbike. God, was I fuming! The bike, his little 'Bella', instantly became an obsession. He cleaned and shined her, photographed her incessantly and took himself off touring at weekends whilst I worked.

"I want to know my new country," he would say.

Then I met Johnny, temporary manager at the hotel. Weekends no longer seemed so dull. He was married but wasn't happy, poor soul! My hours at the hotel increased and Michael suspected nothing.

So there we were, Michael and I, sitting at the kitchen table in spring sunshine drinking coffee, leading far from idyllic lives. The post arrived. Two letters – one for Michael, addressed neatly by hand, and a bill for me. I watched as he opened his. He spent a few moments reading it, looked me square in the eye then dropped his head on his chest. After what seemed like forever, it started!

"Is it true? Is it true, you bitch?" he screamed waving the letter towards me. He leaned across the table until I could feel his breath on my face. My expression must have exposed the truth. He knew. His face was contorted, his eyes stared at me. He got up, threw his chair across the room and stormed from the house. I followed. He ran down the path pausing at the gate to look back at me. He was pale and dishevelled. Then *Michael sat down in the middle of the road and began to cry.* In his hand was the crumpled paper, a letter from Johnny's scorned wife. What had her bitter reaction achieved? If I could get my hands on her...

Johnny proved that he would do anything for me. *On the following Friday we packed our bags and planned our escape.* We drove to the south coast and spent two rainy days in an unexceptional bed and breakfast, gathering ourselves. In one last text from Michael he called me 'an English slut'. That made it much easier for me to move on, I can tell you! *The thing I did to the brakes on the Honda* worried me less with each passing day. Johnny didn't know and it would remain my secret. We jetted out to Spain from Gatwick and were soon settled in our beachside apartment close to Valencia, an exciting new life ahead of us.

"Pop down and get some milk can you, honey?" Johnny called as he turned on the shower. *How lucky am I?* I thought to myself as I wandered down in bright Mediterranean sunshine, the early morning breeze chilling me slightly. I bought milk, some locally grown oranges and a copy of *The Express*.

Back in the apartment the heady scent of Johnny's aftershave filled the air. He was making breakfast so I sat on the balcony reading the paper, when a headline caught my attention.

'Unidentified Body at Crash Scene

Police have been unable to identify the victim of a fatal motorcycle accident. The body of a man,

probably in his thirties and of Caribbean origin, was found at the scene. He was carrying no means of identification but on his left bicep a tattoo, heart-shaped and bearing the initials 'KM'.
Anyone with information…'

Karma

Trisha Todd

Michael sat down in the middle of the road and began to cry. He took a last glance at his car as it turned the corner and disappeared from view, then sobbed harder.

Mr and Mrs Johnson, from number 46, were returning from their daily walk, and dashed across the quiet street to help Michael to his feet. Standing, he brushed bits of black tarmac from his tan corduroy trousers.

"We saw them!" gasped Mrs Johnson as she wound a friendly arm around his waist and walked him to the kerb. "I've never seen the like – that man just pulled you out of your seat and threw you to the ground and the pair of them made off with your car. What is the world coming to?"

"I'll ring the police," Mr Johnson said, fishing in his deep overcoat pocket for his mobile phone.

"Come inside." Mrs Johnson opened her front door and led Michael into the kitchen, sitting him down at her table. She reached for three flowered mugs from the shelf and filled the kettle.

"Nice and strong and sweet – good for shocks," she announced as she placed the coffee in front of him.

Mr Johnson strode through the door and grasped the offered mug.

"Police are on their way," he announced.

Michael stared into the distance through puffy eyes, his face still red from his earlier tears. "I'll never get away," he murmured, shaking his head.

"What's that, dear?" Mrs Johnson placed an age-spotted hand over his and gave a squeeze.

"I'll never get away," he repeated. "I bet she arranged it."

"Arranged what?"

Michael looked from her kindly face to her husband's, and took a deep breath.

"My wife, Lydia; I think she arranged to have my car stolen!"

"Why ever would she do that?" Mr Johnson's bushy brows furrowed in puzzlement.

"Oh, things haven't been good between us for a while now," Michael admitted, running his hand through his dark hair. He paused then, seeming to come to a decision, and continued.

"She barely speaks to me, and when she does it's with another put-down, more abuse. She's a bit quick with her hands too, though I never hit back – that's wrong, hitting a woman. She spread lies about me to our friends, so they don't want to know me – she even rang my boss with some story. I don't know what I'm supposed to have done, but I can't take it anymore, especially after finding her with some other bloke, in our bed!" His voice broke. "She just laughed."

Mrs Johnson nodded, urging him to continue.

"Well, I've found someone else, *and we've been planning our escape – our cases are packed and we were going to leave this Friday* – but now this has happened."

***

Lydia thought she was so clever. *I'll be rid of him soon. Thought I didn't know what he was planning, running away with that stupid cow? Pathetic! Well, she won't get her hands on his money – that insurance payout is all mine, and I'll be set.*

Lydia looked in the mirror and practised her surprised, then upset, look. She shook her blond hair and wiped away her make-up with a tissue. *Wouldn't do to look too beautiful when the police give me the awful news about Michael's demise.*

***

Michael didn't want to go home and so it was some time later that the police car pulled up outside number 46, and two tall, uniformed men got out and walked up the pathway. Mr Johnson let them in and showed them to the kitchen.

"Sorry for the delay. There have been some developments on your case," the younger policemen began. "Your car's been involved in an accident and the two suspected carjackers have been killed."

Michael looked up, shocked.

"Well, what happened?" Mrs Johnson gasped.

"It would appear that the brakes failed as they negotiated the hill out of town. Hit a tree – weren't wearing seat belts, obviously. However, what is interesting is that the scene of crime officers have found the car's been tinkered with. Who's had access to it, and who would want to harm you?" he questioned.

"No, I don't believe it," Michael whispered, shaking his head. In a louder voice he continued. "My wife, Lydia, is the only person with access. The car's been locked in our garage the last few days – she told me she couldn't find the keys and I thought it was just another of her ways to annoy me. *It seems she did things to the brakes of my Honda.*"

***

Lydia didn't need to pretend to look shocked and surprised as the police marched her handcuffed from the house. The police had easily found the hacksaw she had used to cut the brake lines, and she had blurted out the truth.

"Life's just not fair!" she snivelled as she approached the waiting police van.

I cheated on my spouse. And it wasn't the first time.

"If you don't take chances," said the man in striped pyjamas," you might as well not be alive."

The way she made tea.

A Lovely Cup of Tea

Kim Kimber

Last Thursday, I cheated on my spouse. And it wasn't the first time. It was all in aid of science, you realise; I still love George, my husband of twenty-five and a half years, even if our relationship has become a little predictable. We have reached the stage where we can finish each other's sentences. We are comfortable with one another, too comfortable, like a pair of old shoes that you can't possibly get rid of but it might be quite good to try on a new pair occasionally.

Anyway, I am getting ahead of myself. It all started innocently, going back to last spring, when my colleague at the university where I work as an administrator asked me if I would volunteer for her research project. I said yes immediately without even thinking to ask what I would be taking part in. I had helped out before and the topics had mostly involved indulging in my favourite treats to further scientific research; the impact of too much sugar or alcohol, that kind of thing. So, I was looking forward to a pleasant afternoon eating chocolate. I was a little surprised when

I was asked if I could bring along my pyjamas, but these scientists can be a bit eccentric at times.

When I arrived, I was shown into a small cubicle and asked to get changed. Minutes later, dressed in my best M&S flannelettes, I was sat down in a comfy armchair sipping a lovely cup of tea while the research team prepared themselves for the experiment.

Miriam, my colleague, arrived shortly afterwards with her clipboard. "How are you feeling, Jen?" she asked. "Nice and relaxed?"

I nodded happily.

"Good, then we can begin."

I followed Miriam along the corridor into a small room to meet the other participants. Usually, I was one of a large group so it was strange to discover that there was just me and a man in rather magnificent blue and white striped pyjamas. He was taller than me and looked constrained by his PJs, as if he wasn't used to wearing them and couldn't wait to rip them off. I blushed at the thought and offered him my hand to shake but he simply winked cheekily.

"Firstly, thanks for doing this," said Miriam. "You have no idea how difficult it has been finding a couple to agree."

A couple? Now, that was odd. I didn't even know the man's name, so describing us as 'a couple' was going a bit far.

"The bed is all set up in the lab. I think you will find it comfy. I just need to wire you up Jen so that we can monitor your responses."

Bed! I had helped out with quite a lot of projects but had never had to lie down before. Mr stripy PJs was led away by a lab assistant whilst I was fitted with tiny electrodes. Normally, these are located on your arm or head so it was an 'oh my goodness' moment when I felt a hand slip down the waistband of my pyjama trousers and between my thighs. The probe felt cold and clinical, but didn't hurt at all so I happily followed my friend into the research laboratory.

Usually, the lab is bright and littered with instruments and medical paraphernalia but on this occasion, it resembled a cheap hotel room. All the blinds had been pulled down and it was dimly lit, intimate almost. A double bed dominated the centre of the room, where stripy PJs was plumping up pillows and making himself comfortable. He patted the bed next to him as soon as he saw me.

"Go on," encouraged my friend, giving me a little push. "Enjoy yourself."

I lay down on the bed cautiously and immediately felt a strong, muscular arm snake around my waist.

"Ooh, err!" was all I could manage as my partner rolled over in one fluid movement so that he was on top of me. *He's obviously more clued up than I am about this experiment,* I thought to myself a little uneasily.

"Is that really necessary? Have you never heard of personal space? I'm not sure that you're supposed to do that... Is this all a part of the research?" I finally managed to stutter, as his hands roamed around my body. I have to admit the sensation was not unpleasant.

"*If you don't take chances,*" the man in striped pyjamas whispered in my ear, "*you might as well not be alive.*" His breath felt hot on my neck and he smelt pleasantly of cologne. "Time to live a little Jennifer."

"But I'm a married woman…" I protested.

At that moment, an image of George, with his beer belly peeking over the top of his greying Y-fronts, popped into my head. He never smelt of cologne. He was usually vaguely sweaty with a hint of stale cigarettes on his breath, although he claimed to have given up smoking years ago. George's body was rounded and hairy, but the man whose hands were currently exploring my intimate places felt firm and toned.

I tried to stop him. Honestly, I did. *Roam, roam, roam* went his hands… I just really couldn't do this, *probe, probe, probe.* It wouldn't be fair to… oh my, … Geo…rge!

"Stop!" I managed to squeeze out. "Please stop," but my voice came out breathless and husky so that it really didn't sound like me at all.

My partner had, by now, managed to wriggle free of his blue and white striped pyjamas and, well into his stride, didn't appear to hear my feeble protests. Instead he kissed my neck and undid my buttons.

Random thoughts penetrated my hormone saturated brain; *had to stop, not fair on… who? Not fair on… not fair… must stop… the experiment. No! No! I can't stop now, it's research!* I thought triumphantly as the last little bit of my resistance washed away on a tide of pleasure.

Oh, and I nearly forgot to mention… because of the extreme, never-before-recorded results, it has been necessary to repeat the experiment several times, over many months, in and out of the lab.

So, you see, it really wasn't my fault after all. It was all down to my friend and her research. *It was the way she made the tea* that did it, being infused with a new aphrodisiac with hallucinogenic properties that transformed my George from a tubby, middle-aged man into an Adonis. At least in my eyes.

When released on to the market, it is anticipated that the new tea will be bigger than Viagra and me and George will have helped to save flagging libidos and jaded marriages across the UK and beyond.

Unfortunately, the drugs haven't been cleared for use by the general public as yet, so we need to keep on testing for a while longer. One thing is certain; the humble cup of tea has never before been quite so satisfying.

The Session

Lois Maulkin

"*I cheated on my spouse. And it wasn't the first time.*" There, you'd said it. The words were out. The air in the counselling room was thick with them, hanging there, monstrous.

You looked down at your hands, at the twist of damp tissue you held. You gave an enormous sigh. How long had you hidden the admission from yourself, from everyone – from your husband? Long enough for it to gnaw away at the heart of what had been solid and good about the two of you. A tiny noise, like the bicycle bell of a mouse hurrying the gravelly way home from choir practice, sounded somewhere in your head. The thin glass bubble of your marriage shattered, and the air cleared.

"How did it feel?" asked the man in the chair opposite, crossing his slippered feet at the ankles.

"Fantastic," you said dully.

"Why was it 'fantastic'?" he pressed gently. "Could you tell me about it?"

You hadn't expected that. You'd spent so many years squashing the memories away that it was a shock to be asked to unpack them all and look at them again. You got them out. You pulled out the glistening joy and the fear and the shimmering feeling of being loved and the luminous guilt and the excitement and the horror and the ringing, ringing, ringing bliss and you gazed at them and moved them from hand to hand, and then you threw them and splashed them all over the walls, where they bled out into flat patches. You talked him through the maps they made. Did you blush? Just a little?

"Were you looking for excitement? Had you been... perhaps...bored?"

"No, not that," you said firmly. "I just couldn't help it."

You'd been afraid of giving in to an increasing desire to disappear, you told him, to run away, jump on a train or a bus or, or something, and just go. As far as your credit card would take you. Leave everything. Some evenings you had to hold on to the dinner table with both hands to anchor yourself, stop yourself spiralling slowly up on a thermal off the gravy, drifting out of the kitchen, gaining speed along the passageway, surging out of the front door and heading off like a comet to the horizon.

He'd been a reason. A hook. A hand. He'd held you with his flattery and his interest, and like the dreams you got from the doctor's pills, he gave you a fair enough imitation of happiness to make you stay.

You said, "I suppose it was just a chance thing, really."

"If you don't take chances," said the man in striped pyjamas, *"you might as well not be alive."*

"Is that why you've come here without getting dressed?" you asked.

"Have I?" he said, glancing down. "Oh, good God, I do apologise. What on Earth was I thinking?"

"It really doesn't matter," you said, glancing at the clock, and seeing there were just a few minutes left of the allotted hour. "Thank you for listening," you said, blowing your nose and folding your sadness back into your handbag. You sat back in your chair and, drawing a shuddering breath, composed your features into their accustomed arrangement, and said, "So, what brings you to counselling today?"

He looked at you as the buzzer marking the end of the session went, and he rose to go, turning at the door and saying, "I hate myself, Doctor. I drove my wife to suicide going on about *the way she made tea*."

Money for Nothing

Barbara Sleap

I cheated on my spouse and it wasn't the first time either. It all started when I joined the Women's Institute in Weston-on-Sea. The meetings were held in a theatre complex along the seafront and I went to the first meeting with my friend, Mary. My husband gave us both a lift there and then went to visit his mother.

We enjoyed the first two sessions, a fashion show on a proper catwalk and then a cookery demo. However, the third meeting was a Christmas craft evening and, as neither of us fancied making decorative boxes, coloured bows or crackers, Mary suggested we visit the casino where she and her husband had just become members.

I had never been to the casino before. It was only a short walk and we both had a little money for a flutter. I was amazed at the atmosphere inside; it was noisy and crowded, everybody enjoying themselves on different tables, playing blackjack, poker and a complicated looking game called 'craps'. We had a fun time and only just made it back to the Palace Pavilion so that John wouldn't know we'd been elsewhere. I had turned my

£10 into £50 on one of the roulette tables and I felt so good, I couldn't wait to go again.

Mary couldn't make the next month's WI meeting, which was just as well as the evening promised a speaker on bird watching. When John dropped me outside I waited furtively until he had driven away and hurried to the casino where I went through the membership procedure and still had time for the roulette table. I had saved my £50 winnings and spent the whole lot on purple chips. I somehow managed to turn my £50 into £80 this time; it was such a thrilling feeling. I had a huge grin on my face when John picked me up.

"You look like you've won the lottery," he remarked with an innocent smile.

Little did he know!

"Oh, I'm enjoying it so much that I've put my name down for the reading group, you know I've always wanted to join one. They meet here next Thursday."

So the following week after visibly reading *Wolf Hall* which I left in prominent places around the house, I was at the table with £80 worth of pink chips and feeling quite jittery.

After several rounds I was down to my last £10 and feeling despondent. It was a busy evening and a stag party arrived in the bar with the men all wearing pyjamas of various colours. They were quite noisy and one of the party came over to the table and stood next to me. Everyone around the table started laughing.

"Hey, how did you get in dressed like that?" one of the punters asked.

"We're only allowed an hour, then we have to change, it was just a forfeit for the bridegroom. Our real clothes are in the minibus outside, you won't recognise us in an hour's time," he said, giving me a cheeky wink.

He looked down at my diminished pile of chips.

"If you don't take chances," said this man in striped pyjamas, "you might as well not be alive. Fancy taking a chance on me though?"

I stared up at him with a look that sent him shuffling back to his friends in his well-worn furry moccasins. With his words still ringing in my ears I promptly placed my remaining chips on number 22 and waited anxiously. I held my breath as the ball spun round, faltering at number 9 then miraculously bouncing into number 22. I was a winner. At last my luck had changed and after several more rounds I was £150 in profit. However, the clock had caught up with me and by the time I had cashed my chips for crisp notes I had to run like Cinderella after the ball to where John was patiently waiting in the car.

"Enjoy the group? I didn't know reading could make you so puffed," John said, giving me a sideways glance as he pulled into the traffic.

I ignored his remark and asked him if he'd been to see his mum, as usual.

"Oh yes, I certainly did, actually we had a bit of a Barney." I was surprised because John never argued with anybody.

"Why was that?" I asked.

"Well, I criticised *the way she made tea*," he said with a wry grin. This made me laugh because my mother-in-law is renowned for making the worst tea. She uses the cheapest teabags and puts too much UHT milk in the cup. The result is a tepid, greyish liquid which has to be gulped down quickly followed by a firm refusal for a refill.

"Never mind, she'll get over it," I said, "I don't suppose she'll change though."

John nodded in agreement.

"Anyway, you'll be able to find out next week," I added cautiously, "I've joined the WI writing group, and guess what? They meet here next Thursday."

There she was, Amy Gerstein, over by the pool, kissing my father.

She may be young, but she's not stupid.

The day Sheila bought Hillary to my office.

Garden Party

Lois Maulkin

There she was, Amy Gerstein, over by the pool, kissing my father. She was a tough cookie, you had to hand it to her. I wouldn't have kissed him, and he was my father. How she could push her plump, soft lips to his slack-mouthed, scraped looking, cracked face with those slug trails of watery mucus oozing across the bottom half of it I couldn't begin to understand. His head, big as a baby bird's on its fragile, nodding stalk of neck, shone wispily in the sunshine, and Amy Gerstein took his hands in hers and bent to look, smilingly, into his bleary cataracts.

"Timothy," she said, her voice sparkling across the pool. "Timothy, it's lovely to see you looking so well."

My mother came out of the house just then, attempting elegance in her best clothes, the heels of her Autograph sandals sinking into the lawn.

"Amy!" she called brightly. "Amy, hello, how good of you to come."

"Sheila, I wouldn't have missed it for the world." Amy Gerstein straightened up and watched my mother progress down the long slope of the garden, divots flying with each step. "I was just saying to Timothy how well he looks."

"The doctors say he's doing very well," lied my mother, "he's better every day, aren't you, Timbo?" She took hold of the handles of his wheelchair, "Time for a nap now though," and set off with him back towards the French windows. It was heavy going. The combination of soft grass, heels, wheels and wobbling head made a spectacle it was impossible not to watch, and for some time, perhaps as long as five minutes, the guests stared as one. As the opening strains of Elgar's 'Nimrod' meandered across the summer afternoon, my mother ploughed across the garden, her company smile slowly giving way to a grimace as she gritted her dentures and bent lower, arms outstretched, head down and pushed stoically on.

"Pull it, Sheila," murmured Hillary Benson.

Hillary's words seemed to break some kind of spell, and suddenly, or as suddenly as elderly guests tend to move on a warm August afternoon with Pimm's on their breath and little bits of mint stuck round their mouth, several of them took off to assist. Mother knocked the wheelchair into one of them, and he fell down, but it was only Ted Nubis, who everyone agreed was an insufferable buffoon, and he apologised for getting in the way. He was helped up by Amy Gerstein who dusted him off and sat him in one of the little golden chairs mother had hired for the occasion. Eventually, Brian

Samuels wrestled the wheelchair from mother, and she was persuaded to sit, smiling grimly, wheezing and perspiring, in another little golden chair while Amy Gerstein, youth personified, fetched a glass of water and an asthma pump.

"Such a beautiful party, Sheila," she said, looking out across the flower beds to where Brian and Hillary were pulling the wheelchair up the slope towards the patio.

"Shall we take him right in?" shouted Brian Samuels to my mother. There was a scent of decay coming from my father, which cut across the perfumes of the rose beds and the smoked salmon, and I realised Mother had thrown the party now as it was probably the last time my father would be acceptable in company. It sounds harsh, but I know the way her mind works.

"Yes please, Brian," said mother. "Just leave him at the foot of the stairs and I'll pop him on the Stannah when I've got my breath back."

"Let me do that," said Amy Gerstein, strolling with an easy briskness in through the French windows.

"Will she manage?" asked Ted, watching her long brown hair swinging.

"*She may be young but she's not stupid,*" said my mother, her voice just on the right side of testy.

At that moment, there was a scream, a clatter, and a muted groan, and my father's wheelchair shot out of the French windows, with Amy Gerstein sprinting after it.

Across the patio they hurtled, my father's head bobbing wildly as the chair gained speed, and Amy Gerstein kicking off her shoes to run faster.

"Good Lord," said Ted Nubis as he tottered from his seat and fell over. My mother heaved herself up, rolling her eyes and stepping across Ted, and joined the herd of other guests who took off down the garden as fast as their assorted medical complaints would allow.

With a wail and a splash the wheelchair entered the pool, and Amy Gerstein leapt in after it. There was an agonising wait while Amy dived...twice...three times... and again...to locate the chair, release the safety belt and haul my father up to the surface, and then Brian Samuels and Ted Nubis dragged him out, and laid him on the side of the pool. Amy Gerstein, once again demonstrating admirable steeliness, administered resuscitation and everyone watched, one or two people sobbing quietly.

"Call an ambulance," yelled my mother, and Ted started patting his suit pockets looking for his phone.

"It's here somewhere," he said, tapping his thighs. "I know it is."

"Too late, old boy," murmured Hillary Benson.

***

That evening, Amy Gerstein and I sat in the piano bar of the Wifebeater's Arms Hotel.

"I feel awful," she said, sighing, and opening a bag of cheese and onion crisps.

"You mustn't," I said, pushing a lock of her hair gently back from her face and holding her soft, warm cheek in my hand. "Everyone could see it was a terrible accident. The brakes on his wheelchair had obviously been going for ages," I took a crisp, "and you really did all you could to help him. No one could have done more."

"Do you think everyone thought that?"

"Of course! And what's more, the way Dad was going, it really was a kindness for all concerned, my love."

We sat quietly for a moment, sipping our drinks, and finishing off the crisps. Amy licked her fingers. "And of course the financial aspect – well, we can do it now. Hillary Benson is a brilliant accountant, and it's all worked out to the last perfect little penny." Amy's face took on the beautiful, heavy-eyed, dreamy look it always wore when she thought about money, and I felt my heart flutter happily, shifting itself deeper down into the warm red nest of my love for her.

"Yes, Amy," I said, "Tenderlings, our own care home. We can look after the whole mad bunch of them." I picked up my drink and settled further back into the white leather sofa. "Tell me again how you and Mother thought of it."

"Well," said Amy Gerstein, pulling my arm around her and snuggling in to me. "*It all started the day Sheila brought Hillary to my office.*"

The Sins of the Father

Sue Duggans

Amy Gerstein had been the 'goody two shoes' of my class throughout junior school. Platinum blonde plaits, bows, shiny shoes, good at everything; a classic teacher's pet!

Then, she moved to Hampton Girls' Grammar along with my adored best friend, Katie Junior, Julie Hetherington and me.

"She's such a sweet girl," my mother cooed after we met Amy with her intensely irritating mother at the school's open day in July. "We must invite her for a sleepover during the holidays, darling."

"Over my dead body," I mumbled to myself.

As luck would have it, Amy and her doting parents were away for the whole of August. Instead, I invited Katie and what a sleepover that was! We went out and blew our pocket money on sugar-laden goodies. We secreted our stash in my attic bedroom then joined my parents for dinner. After a game of Scrabble, Katie and I wasted no time in getting off to bed. We giggled, as schoolgirls do, gorged on sugar and gasped and guffawed over some filthy magazines which I'd uncovered in my father's study when I should have been researching the significance of Hadrian's Wall. We were shocked that girls, not much older than ourselves, would allow themselves to be photographed that way and surprised that a respectable man like my father would want to look at them! We slept well that night, Katie and I, despite the sugar.

The next day we went to town to see a film at the local cinema. This was particularly memorable for me as it was the first time I'd been allowed to go to the cinema without an adult. The film, however, was less memorable and its title escapes me.

***

That was all ten years ago.

My parents separated in my final term at Durham. During my university years I hadn't returned home much, only for main holidays and special occasions, such was the lure of independence and a hugely hedonistic lifestyle! My mother's sister, Aunt Sheila, phoned to tell me that my father had left following his admission of an eighteen month affair with a young social climber more than half his age. My father was a successful solicitor and senior partner in his practice. *She* was employed there.

My determination to get a first in History (Hadrian's Wall having inspired me more than I could have dreamed!) prevented me from absorbing the full impact that my father's affair and departure would have on my mother. Thank heavens for Aunt Sheila, who proved to be a stalwart for Mum and well-practised in dealing with the fallout from love-rats!

I returned home in June, having achieved my first, and was happy to move back to my attic bedroom and give my mother much-needed moral support and company. I chose to have no contact with my father. My heart had hardened towards him.

Following a successful interview, Aunt Sheila's current partner, the silky-smooth Simon, offered me a job in his publishing company. I knew it probably wouldn't be long term but it suited for the time being.

Katie, recently returned from university in York, and I began to meet up regularly and decided towards the end of August to join the newly-opened health spa. Our slightly skewed logic was that swimming, saunas and the occasional gym session would counteract our regular weekend binging!

Our first visit was on a hot Saturday afternoon prior to a routine night out. We'd both splashed out on new training bags and filled them with expensive kit, most of which would, no doubt, rarely be used! We changed into our bikinis ready for a not-too-strenuous swim and made our way to the outdoor pool. The sun was hot as we stepped onto the overcrowded patio area but we were not deterred. As we snaked our way through the crowd towards the pool steps I glanced up and *there she was,*

Amy Gerstein, over by the pool, kissing my father. He was gazing down at her like a love-struck teenager. I felt sick.

"*She might be young but she's not stupid!* I always thought she had the makings of a gold digger." Katie spoke in a disapproving tone. She was not wrong.

Amy hadn't gone to university but stayed at home where she was indulged by her parents and, rumour had it, smooth talked and flattered by a string of wealthy, eligible men.

When my father spotted me he held me in his gaze for some moments then whispered in Amy's ear, took her hand and led her away. Amy didn't look up.

***

They say revenge is sweet! My revenge of sorts was inflicted on Amy's mother, Hillary Gerstein, in a strange and ironic reversal of 'The Sins of the Father'. She applied for a part-time post at Simon's company and, as the successful applicant would be working closely with me, I was invited by Simon and Sheila to join the interview panel. I had made my mark in the company and was enjoying learning more about the various aspects of publishing. I had my own office and, with a rapidly increasing workload, Simon decided to provide me with a part-time assistant. Three applicants were shortlisted.

The day Sheila brought Hillary to my office for interview was the day I knew that revenge can be sweet. She recognised me straight away and at once began to justify Amy's decision to sidestep university. It was clearly a defence strategy – she could barely hide her disappointment. It was no surprise that her daughter's living and sleeping with my father wasn't mentioned. Sheila, every bit the proud aunt as well as being privy to the grubby goings-on in the life of the Gerstein girl, told Hillary that I'd achieved a first at Durham. Hillary's smile and congratulations left me unmoved although may well have been genuine.

The interview began! Sheila and I took turns to fire the questions:

"Why did you apply for the post?"

"What key qualities will you bring to the role?"

"What is your approach to finding solutions to difficult situations?"

"What are your views on personal relationships between members of staff?" This one was not scripted. I'd thrown it in myself. When I asked the question I was conscious of Sheila's sideways glance in my direction. Had I overstepped the mark?

Hillary moved uneasily and fumbled with the buttons on her neat cardigan. Her face was flushed at the end of the interview. She was not unintelligent and had answered well, considering.

The job went to Liz Morgan, a slightly eccentric woman with three teenaged kids and bags of personality as well as an enviable knowledge of both French and English literature. I looked forward to working with her.

Sheila phoned her with the good news and I had the unenviable job of phoning the others. "Mrs Gerstein. I'm sorry to say that you've been unsuccessful at interview. However, I'd like to thank you for attending and wish you well."

I resisted the temptation to add, "Say hello to Amy and my father when you see them."

Pool Party

Josephine Gibson

"*There she was, Amy Gerstein, over by the pool, kissing my father.*"

He paused and stared out of the window for a moment, looking at the sky.

"It was that long, hot summer of '76. Do you remember it?"

When I murmured, "No," he continued.

"Perhaps not, you look a little young. For me – I was sixteen – it felt like a once-in-a-generation event. The TV and newspapers were full of it; the drought and how to cope. My father and I used to fill buckets with bath water after the girls had finished and use it to water the garden. Taking showers wasn't as popular then as it is now.

"Anyway, that summer we had to be really careful to conserve the water in the swimming pool – no dive bombing or boisterous games, my father had said.

"The pool was great – only small – but we had a changing hut at one end and a seating area at the other. It had a pergola covered with clambering roses. I can still remember sitting there, the sound of the filter flapping –

breaking that stillness after we'd finished swimming. The feeling of the rough paving slabs underfoot as you ran around the pool. We had a lot of fun there as kids. My father used to float in a big rubber tyre and we'd try to dislodge him. It would take all four of us to tip him out.

"Good times," he sighed.

"By the time I was sixteen I was using the pool for other activities. Huh, it doesn't take much to imagine what a red-blooded teenage boy spent most of his time thinking about and planning. The pool was a great attraction; it made me seem cool to be able to invite girls around for a swim. I'd tell them to get dropped off at the bottom of the lane which meant we were spared the embarrassment of our mothers meeting, and I used to enjoy their doe eyed look when they saw the size of the property. When they realised the lane they'd just walked up actually belonged to me.

"So, Amy; I'd thought she was out of my league, one of the grammar school girls. A big group of us would meet at the bus stop after school. She seemed sophisticated, wore a lot of make-up, had this gorgeous blonde hair – a bit like Agnetha, the glamorous one from ABBA. Oh, Agnetha," he sighed, "she fuelled a few of my teenage fantasies...

"My strategy for Amy was to target the best friend, and once Jenny had been around a couple of times and boasted about the house and pool, Amy had to prove she was prettier and started to flirt outrageously. Poor Jenny – ha! No clue.

"So, that long, hot afternoon, I'd arranged the seduction of Amy Gerstein. My mother and sisters were out shopping and the house was my own. I'd prepared a big jug of Pimm's complete with the trimmings – mint and strawberry from the garden. Pimm's was pretty unusual in those days but at my age and in my social circle, my parents expected me to be able to entertain and didn't object to me drinking. Obviously, I'd filched the best cut tumblers as I had a guest. Well, I hoped to have her...sorry, cheap joke."

No one had laughed.

"Amy changed into a bikini and after a swim we lay on the sun loungers at the end of the pool, pretending we were something out of *Great Gatsby*. You know, I still remember that afternoon. The heat, the warmth of her damp skin under my hand, her cool lips and the taste of alcohol when I kissed her. It was all so innocent; we were sixteen, for God's sake.

"I don't know how far I would have got if a tumbler hadn't been knocked over. Like an idiot I stepped on the broken glass and gashed my foot. I left her alone to go inside for a plaster, the phone rang and I had to take a message for my mother – and when I came back that's when I found my father and Amy.

"That old goat! I hadn't even known he was around and I think he must have been spying on us, probably from the shed where the chlorine was kept. What sort of person watches a couple of teenagers snogging? He must have made his move pretty quickly after I'd gone indoors – probably used cleaning up the mess as an excuse to saunter over to Amy and show some interest in her studies or some such. She was quite drunk by then – the Pimm's had worked, hadn't it – and I guess he surprised her and made a pass at her.

"I don't know how he did it but it spoiled the party and she made an excuse and left soon after. My only satisfaction was the thought she'd have to walk a couple of miles to find the nearest phone box.

"I can't tell you how angry I was. It was probably the booze. That was the first time I went for my father, and I can tell you, it was pretty humiliating. He was still stronger than me then and he got me in a headlock. While I was struggling he decided to tell me a few home truths about women and how to seduce them.

"'*She may be young, but she's not stupid,*' he said of Amy, boasting how his power and status acted as an aphrodisiac. I felt sick to the stomach, an innocent boyhood adventure ruined.

"That was the day my childhood ended. He decided to induct me into his playboy world of casual pickups and affairs that I'd never imagined. He told me my mother knew about them and it was part of the contract between them. He provided her with the lifestyle, she provided him with children and a comfortable home, and she jolly well turned a blind eye to his adventures or risk losing everything. He said she preferred it that way; women like her didn't like sex much.

"I felt so betrayed by both of them and the lies they'd lived.

"And to add insult to injury, he told me not to worry about Amy, he'd take me up to Soho and show me a good time. A promise he kept – and my mother never stopped him.

"I honestly think he wanted to make me in his image and..." he paused for a long time, tears filling his eyes, then said, his voice cracking, "and I think to a large extent he succeeded.

"And you know what? You know what?" he shouted, "I've felt so lonely most of my life and none of it, none of it," he looked up and swept his arms to mentally push away his surroundings, "nothing that I've got or I've earned, or the women I've slept with, none of it means anything if Sheila leaves me."

He was silent. Sheila and I sat, and I listened to the ticking clock. I took a breath and prepared myself to see if there was anything I could do to help them deal with the affairs and the betrayals, the self-pity and self-justification, whether Hillary could change and whether Sheila could forgive him. *That was the day Sheila brought Hillary to my office.*

Include the following words in a story or poem:

Umbrella, Goldfish bowl, Reading glasses, Broom, Oil painting, Mirror

(Words by WoSWI Writing Group)

Forever Young

Barbara Sleap

I'm no *oil painting* now at sixty-eight,
When I look in the *mirror* the wrinkles I hate.
I've tried all the creams to help fill them in,
But the jars and tubes just end up in the bin.

The TV is no more than a *goldfish bowl*,
Showing flawless models, not a spot or a mole,
Under an *umbrella* or lying in the sun,
So lithe, tanned and slim, so full of fun.

Getting old gives a feeling of oncoming doom,
This image I'd like to sweep with a *broom*.
Throw out my *glasses*, flat shoes and run
'Cos I want to be beautiful and forever young.

Moving Mum

Kim Kimber

"Mum..." I say, nudging her gently, "are you okay?"

"Hmmm, yes, sorry, my mind must have wandered. I was just remembering when I got this *umbrella*. Your dad bought it for me. We were on holiday in Scarborough. It was supposed to be a romantic break, just the two of us, but the weather was terrible; rained all the time. Your dad ran into a little shop and came out carrying this." She holds up the remnants of an umbrella. Light shines through holes in the ripped fabric and half the spokes are missing.

"I don't think it would keep off much rain now," I laugh, taking it from her and tossing it on the rubbish pile. She looks hurt and not for the first time this morning.

"Oh, I couldn't possibly part with it," she insists, grabbing it back with surprising strength for someone so frail. "It holds a special memory."

"So does most of this stuff according to you," I say more jovially than I feel. I look around the room in despair; the 'to keep' pile is now double the size of both the 'charity' and 'bin' boxes and growing. "The idea is to clear things out, Mum," I say gently, "you haven't missed this umbrella for years and it serves no use, why would you want to keep it?"

I know the answer, even before she gives me 'the look', the one that says 'because I want to... because you are discarding my treasured possessions along with my feelings and forcing me to move away from my home'.

Exactly when I became the enemy, I can't remember for sure. I can recall endless conversations over the phone with my sister, Ellie, in Canada about how Mum was struggling to cope and what *we* should do about it. And then the long line of carers who came to help but Mum drove away, one by one, until they refused to visit anymore. Mum even threw her dinner at one of them, for reasons which are still not clear although I did make out the words 'bib', 'mess' and 'for her own good' from the hysterical woman on the other end of the phone.

Mum's tolerance of others seemed to disappear with her ability to look after herself and, the more apparent it became that she needed help, the less willing she was to accept it. Her choices dwindled along with the years and now here we are boxing up her things in readiness for the big move.

"Come on," I say, "let's take a break. I'll make us some tea."

When I enter the room with a tray containing two steaming mugs of tea and a plate of biscuits, Mum is sat with a *goldfish bowl* over her head.

I drop the tray, tea slopping everywhere, and rush over to help her.

"It won't come off," says a muffled voice from underneath the glass dome. Her breath steams up the inside as I start to pull.

I tug hard and the bowl releases its grip in a rush, sending me tumbling backwards. Mum laughs and I can't help joining in now that the emergency has passed. "You could make money on YouTube, pulling stunts like that," I say.

"What's a U-tube?" Mum asks looking puzzled. "Is it like a U-bend? I wouldn't want to get stuck in one of those. Too smelly! Do you remember that goldfish you won at the fair? You couldn't get the hoops over the squares and your dad ended up paying over the odds to buy one of the fish for you. He said it would be dead in a week but it lived for years."

"Of course I do," I say, getting up and handing her a mug of tea. "Goldfin, after the villain, Goldfinger, Dad loved all those old Bond films. That fish was still swimming around long after I left for university but, Mum, what were you doing with the bowl on your head?"

"I wanted to see how it would feel, living in a confined space, hemmed in with no escape. That will be me soon."

"You'll have your own room, you know that. And it's a new start for you in a lovely place, one where you will be safe and looked after."

"Safe is boring," she says, sipping her tea noisily.

"Did you even look at the brochure? Now where did it go?" I look around and eventually locate the glossy booklet at the bottom of the paper recycling pile. "This is not rubbish, Mum," I say sternly, dropping it on to her lap.

"Can I have a biscuit?" Mum asks spying the chocolate coated digestives – her favourites – "and then I'll look at your damn brochure. But you'll have to find my *reading glasses*, or I won't be able to see a thing."

* * *

Several hours later, we still haven't located the missing glasses although I have found a cracked *mirror*, several odd shoes, a stack of battered books, a box of chipped cups and saucers and several loose jigsaw puzzle pieces.

I almost suspect that Mum has hidden her glasses on purpose. The brochure for Sunnydays Retirement Home lies unopened next to her, as she dozes in her chair. Her mouth is open and she snores softly, her chest rising and falling steadily, like a well-oiled piston. I am exhausted, mentally and physically, and wish that I too could lie back on the settee and pretend this wasn't happening. She looks peaceful, her lined face showing no sign of the stress we have put her under of late; us traitors, her daughters.

Right on cue, the phone rings, "Hi, how's it going?" My sister's pseudo-Canadian drawl comes over the line.

"Not well, Ellie," I confess, studying a pile of faded *oil paintings* stacked in the corner of the room and wondering why I'd never seen any of them before. Next to them is a bigger pile of old black and white photographs, the subjects enlarged and immortalised in dusty frames. Spooky images of long-dead relatives stare back at me accusingly.

"It was never going to be easy, sis, but it's the right thing to do."

The right thing for you, I think to myself, *thousands of miles away and free from responsibility.*

"It's just that she is so set against it."

"Of course she is, bound to be, it's a big change but what is the alternative? She can't very well fly out to Canada and you can't look after her, not in your condition. How is my new niece anyway?"

I rub my swollen belly, confirmed as being a girl on the same day that I accepted Mum's place at the home. A daughter, whom I already know that I would gladly die for. Would she too be sitting in my position, years from now, packing me off to a home, discarding me along with the piles of rubbish?

I remember Mum's face when I told her the news about the baby, how happy she was to be having a grandchild at last. Ellie lives in Canada with her girlfriend, a butch woman called Jet whom we had met only once, but whose appearance confirmed beyond doubt my sister's preferences in a partner.

After a succession of failed relationships, I had myself given up on the idea of ever having a child. Time after time, Mum had provided tea and tissues as my latest boyfriend left me. My current situation came about as a result of a one night stand at a conference in London after making too good use of the free bar. It was hardly the dream start that I had hoped for, but as I sat on the bathroom floor clutching the little piece of plastic that told me I was indeed pregnant, I couldn't help feeling excited. I was forty-three years of age and about to embark on the biggest adventure of my life, and the most important; motherhood.

"Sorry," I say, snapping back to the present and Ellie calling long distance on the end of the phone. "I've got to go, there's a lot still to do, maybe you could call back later. I'll text you when Mum wakes up." I drop the phone, feeling suddenly energised, grab the *broom*, and set to work.

* * *

"Mum, wake up," I say, shaking her, "come on."

"What..." she looks at me in confusion, her face clouding over as she focusses on the stack of boxes, now lined up neatly against the wall, ready to throw out or take to the charity shop.

"I must have dozed off," she says and I laugh.

"You've been asleep for hours. Ellie phoned and I said that you would speak to her later. They are eight hours behind us in Canada so there is still time. Are you feeling better?"

I sit down beside her and hold her hand, as she has done mine on so many occasions in the past.

"I don't want to leave my home," she says.

"I know, maybe you won't have to," I say, inhaling deeply, "there may be another solution. I could move in here with you? There's more space now that we have cleared out all that junk. It will save money as I'm going to have to stop working for a while."

"I'd like that," she whispers, "but I don't think I'd be a lot of help with the baby. You'd have your hands full with two of us to look after. I'm old and useless and you're right to lock me away."

"I want to do this, Mum," I say, certain now that it is the right thing for all of us. A little foot gives me a firm kick and I place Mum's hand on my tummy so that she can feel the new life inside of me. "And I think that your granddaughter agrees."

I know it won't be easy with two demanding females to care for; one life just starting, another in the final years, but nothing worth doing ever is. I will make it work somehow, I owe it to the woman who has always cared for me and for the child I will soon be welcoming into both our lives.

The Locket

A collaboration project

We were honoured when Karen Maitland, author of *The Falcons of Fire and Ice* and, incidentally, a really lovely woman, came to visit WoSWI. During her talk, Karen mentioned that she is part of a group of authors who write stories linked by a common theme.

Inspired, those of us in the writing group decided it would be fun to do something similar and, having chosen a locket to base our stories around, we all picked a decade to set our story in, and went away to write.

We are still surprised at how something that seemed so simple in theory could grow into something so bizarrely tricky in practice. It was like a version of the chaos theory. Someone would notice a tiny change which had to be made to one story, and everyone else's had to alter correspondingly.

Meeting after meeting, over gallons of tea and mountains of biscuits and, on one or two particularly knotty occasions, enough wine to make it all drift off into the sunset, we read and wrote and groaned our way through plot impossibilities, sisters who disappeared, mothers who could never have existed, jobs which people didn't have, 'imposter' lockets coming and going, name changes, age changes, misremembered childhoods, things changing colour, and had an absolute blast!

And so, here it is, a group of stories based around a locket, and if you can read it without being reminded of so much unravelling knitting, we will be more than happy.

Joanie's Locket

Kim Kimber

Wolverhampton, 1940

Darling Harry

I am at the church where only a few short days ago we stood at the altar and made our vows. We were so lucky to get that special licence to marry before you had to go away.

I feel close to you here perched on a wooden pew in solitude. I wish that I could somehow capture this calm and wrap it up like a blanket so that we could throw it over the whole of Europe and extinguish the madness that has overtaken us all.

It is packed at home at the moment and this is the only place I can get any peace to write to you. Mary and Jane have both moved back home while Frank and Jim are away in the army so it's a bit of a squeeze but I know that I shouldn't complain.

It was terrible seeing you off on that overcrowded train. I was convinced that you would all die of suffocation long before you reached the barracks. It was sad to see you looking so handsome in the uniform you wore to get married, wearing it again to go off and fight in a war that none of us asked for. It was good of you to be so cheerful when you knew my own selfish heart was breaking. Your cheeky smile was the last thing I saw as the train pulled away from the platform.

I am wearing the locket you gave me. It hangs just above my heart and I will never take it off as long as I live. I don't know where you managed to find such a beautiful gift in these difficult times and I hope that you have not gone without to pay for it.

I have to go now, my love, or I will miss the trolleybus and I am due for my shift at the factory. Some of the men who remain still resent our presence, although they tend to play tricks on us girls rather than act out of malice. One of them asked Mary if she could go to the stores and fetch him a new bubble for his spirit level. How they all laughed when she came back red-faced and empty-handed.

I will write again tomorrow. In the meantime, stay safe and remember that I carry you with me always.

Your loving wife,
Joan *x*

***

Egypt, 1940

My Dearest Joanie

I am glad that you are safe, your daily letters keep me going, although they arrive erratically, often all together and then nothing at all for days. Just make sure that you continue to number them, so that I can read them in order. And how wonderful it is when I have a batch to read.

I won't lie to you; it is hot and horrible here. The flies are everywhere and we have to shake out our boots every morning in case there are scorpions hiding in them. Our tent is basic and the dust gets everywhere but me and the lads are finding ways to make it more comfortable. The camaraderie makes the hardship more tolerable.

We have been bombed. I'm fine so don't worry, I sheltered under my truck – not the most sensible place seeing as it was full of munitions but I was lucky this time. I'm not allowed to tell you more and even this much may be cut by the censors.

I'm glad you like the locket so much. I bought it in a jewellers, tucked away in a backstreet of Birmingham, shortly before the wedding. It caught my eye because the vivid blue of the flower reminds me of the colour of your eyes. The jeweller said it would always bring us luck.

I have to go now my love, but I will write as soon as I can.

Keep safe for me.
Harry *xx*

***

POST OFFICE
TELEGRAM
Wolverhampton 1940

CONGRATULATIONS
ON THE BIRTH OF A DAUGHTER,
ELIZABETH JOAN
BORN 14 NOVEMBER, 1940 7LBS 6OZS
MOTHER AND BABY DOING WELL.

***

Wolverhampton, December 1940

Darling Harry

I hope that you got the photo of me with Elizabeth. It was so difficult to arrange and send but if it reaches you, the trouble and expense will have been worth it.

I am told by everyone how fortunate I am; Elizabeth is a good baby, and she seldom cries. She is certainly bonny and putting on weight, although it is a great effort to feed her and I just don't seem to have the energy. Poor Ma has her hands full, with an extra person in the house to look after and me still not able to do much. She has been so good. I don't know what we would all do without her.

How are you? It is cold and dark here, sometimes it feels like it is perpetually night but I guess the blackout makes everyone feel that way. It is hard for me to imagine what it must be like in the heat of the desert. Our worlds are so very different at the moment. I wish that this terrible war would end soon and our boys could all come home. Maybe this time next year, we can be together as a family, I can only hope and pray for that time to come soon. Ma is trying her best to make Christmas jolly for everyone but I cannot shake off the feeling of dread as it approaches and I am constantly miserable. I can't bear the thought of Christmas Day without you.

Your letters are less frequent and I imagine it is difficult for you to write, but it is hard for me to remain positive when there is so little news.

Please write soon. I miss you.

Joan and Elizabeth *xx*

POST OFFICE
TELEGRAM
War Office December 1940

I DEEPLY REGRET TO INFORM YOU THAT YOUR HUSBAND 568254 L CPL THOMPSON, H. WENT MISSING FROM OUR OPERATIONS ON 20 DECEMBER AND IS PRESUMED DEAD. PLEASE ACCEPT OUR PROFOUND SYMPATHY PENDING WRITTEN NOTIFICATION.

***

Christmas Day 1940

My dearest Elizabeth

I am sorry to be writing this letter to you, but there is no other way. I hope one day, when you are older, you will understand.

Your father, Harry, is missing, presumed dead and I cannot go on without him. I love him so much. I have proved to be a poor mother, locking myself away and ignoring your cries, and it is your grandma who has cared for you as if you were her own. I know that she will be there for you. She will not fail you as I have.

I wish that things could have been different but I cannot shake off these dark feelings. I can't eat or sleep and I am anxious all of the time. The only way I will find peace is to be with Harry.

I am leaving you the locket your dad gave to me on our wedding day. Keep it safe, close to your heart, and we will always be near.

I know that you will grow up to be a wonderful woman, Elizabeth. Be good for your grandma and please try to forgive me.

I am with you now and always.

Your loving mother *x*

Pandora's Box

Trisha Todd

Elizabeth

Elvis Presley's 'Shake, Rattle and Roll' rocked out of the radio as Elizabeth perched on the edge of her bed, staring at the box in her lap, at the neat writing.

My dearest Elizabeth, from your Mother. The *x* at the end looked hastily added, an afterthought. Ten minutes ago, Elizabeth had been happily enjoying her birthday; having turned fifteen, she had felt very grown up. Now a frown creased her forehead as she chewed her bottom lip, staring at the small, battered box she had been given, apprehensive at what it may contain.

Elizabeth knew that she was adopted – she thought back to when she was five and due to start school. Her father had sat her on his lap and told her, in his deep, soft voice, that she was a special girl and had been given to them to love. When she was better able to understand, he told her they'd known her grandma for years and that she had left Elizabeth with them after admitting she couldn't cope with another baby 'at her time of life'. It was true; the toll of Joan's suicide had caught up with her a few months later and she now lay at rest in the ground next to her daughter.

Elizabeth was a happy child, though times were hard. She was an intelligent girl, easily coping with the demands of the three Rs at school and decided quite early on that she would be a nurse, applying herself to her studies. She was often in her room with her head in a book, her radio playing the latest hit, rather than out with friends. Now she sat in that room, fingers brushing the box edges, hesitant to open the lid.

With trembling fingers, she pulled at the faded red ribbon, sneezing at the little cloud of dust released. A single sheet of Basildon Bond paper lay upon the tissue paper. Afraid to breathe, she picked it up, unfolding it to read the neat writing that lined the page.

Joan's letter brought tears to Elizabeth's eyes and she dabbed at them with her handkerchief before putting the page aside and opening the crumpled tissue. After all the years, the locket was tarnished in places though the blue flowers remained vivid. Inside, she found tiny photographs and, squinting, could just make out a handsome man and a pretty woman – her birth parents. She undid the clasp and hung the locket carefully around her neck; she'd ask her mother to help her polish it later.

***

Harry

He had woken in the military hospital with his head in bandages, a patch over his left eye and plaster casts over his legs. He didn't know who he was, where he'd been or what had happened, only that he was quite happy to be lying there.

The nursing staff filled in some of the blanks, using the papers that were found with him. He was warm and fed and, much later, learned to walk again, although always with a limp. His mental state was not so easily rectified and he was sent to the countryside to convalesce until the doctors were satisfied that he was well enough to return home.

Home was not, however, how he had imagined it whilst in hospital. Most of the street had taken a hit from a bombing raid, and the rebuilding was slow. He was relieved at first to find the house still standing. He knocked at number 84 to find a different family living there. They briefly explained what had happened to the previous occupants, comforting him when he realised Joan was dead. They couldn't say what had happened to Elizabeth, and so he began his hunt.

It was a difficult task, trying to locate old neighbours and people who might have known the family and what had become of Elizabeth, across town and beyond, those who survived anyway. From the details they were able to give him, he tried to piece together the clues and over the next few years he travelled across the country, working where he could, but without success.

He was making yet another search of yet another town. It was market day – rationing had recently ended and the streets were crowded with shoppers; ladies in tweed coats, scarves wrapped around permed hairdos, shopping bags swinging; small boys, their dark shorts showing scraped knees as they raced amongst the stalls pretending to be fighter pilots; dogs sniffing the pavements, hoping to find scraps.

He pushed his way through the people, weary, when a young girl squeezed past in the opposite direction. *Pretty young thing*, he thought, as at the last moment he caught sight of a silver chain and a flash of a blue-flowered locket around her slender neck. Spinning round as quickly as he could manage on his gammy leg, he searched for the girl – but she was nowhere to be seen.

Lost and Found

Barbara Sleap

He was positive he had just seen Elizabeth in a crowded street. It must have been her; the resemblance to the photo of her mother was uncanny. Had he found her after all this time? He had been searching for her since returning from the war and discovering not only that Joanie was dead but that Elizabeth had been adopted. He had, only by chance, glimpsed the distinctive blue and silver locket this girl had been wearing but she had disappeared into the crowd.

His war injuries made him slow and unsteady on his feet so when someone accidentally pushed passed him he tripped down the kerb in front of an oncoming car. As he lay in the road surrounded by a crowd of shocked onlookers, a young woman ran from a nearby coffee bar and crouched over the dazed man. She quickly called out that she was a nurse and asked someone to telephone for an ambulance. As she turned towards her patient her silver locket glinted in the sun…

***

Ten years later, Harry sat in his little patch of garden with a cup of tea reflecting on his life, the past and the future.

He gave a long sigh; for some reason he felt very weary today. Since he had found Elizabeth, his life had positively turned around and it was all due to that little silver locket. Luckily, he hadn't been badly hurt in the road accident. He had sat in hospital afterwards chatting with Elizabeth and listening while she told him the story of her childhood.

Elizabeth was cared for as a baby by her elderly grandmother, then lived with her adoptive parents following her mother's suicide. She had been happy but, nevertheless, had always felt that something in her life was missing. Elizabeth's husband, Max, had whisked her off her feet and filled some of the void but she had always kept a part of herself protected and untouchable. So she had believed in Harry and seemed keen for him to be part of her family.

Elizabeth had welcomed Harry unconditionally and had helped him to buy his small ground floor flat, a luxury for Harry whose old war wounds still caused him pain and discomfort. She had bought him his little car with some of the money she inherited when her adoptive parents died within months of each other. It was only a Hillman Imp but it got him to and from his part time job in a local hardware shop and to visit his 'girlfriend', Paula.

He and Paula had spent a lot of time together since their first meeting at the shop and had quickly become a couple. Paula had a son, Gerry, who had emigrated to Australia on the £10 scheme a few years back, and she and Harry had been saving up for a visit. Paula was obviously longing to see Gerry, his wife and their son but Harry felt a little daunted about having to meet them all, it was a big commitment.

However, the most precious thing Elizabeth had brought into his life was his granddaughter, Julie; she was his pride and joy. He had loved picking her up from nursery school and taking her home for fish fingers and chips or to the local Wimpy Bar for a cheeseburger and a milk shake. Now she was at school and, as well as collecting her, he often attended her school events as a proud grandfather. Elizabeth was kept busy as a part time nurse. Her days involved her work on the medical ward at the hospital and a couple of afternoons a week at a local day centre for old folk with fading memories. She was always busy and Harry was so proud of her.

Things had changed, though, when Elizabeth had come to him in tears a few weeks ago and confessed that she had lost her beloved locket. She and Max had searched everywhere; the house, their car and her places of work. She had also reported the loss to the police, just in case. Harry had felt so sorry for Elizabeth and he hated seeing her upset, so, rightly or wrongly, he and Paula had visited a small, specialist jeweller in town and the clever young man there had made a replica. Of course, nothing could replace the original but the chap had made an excellent job of it considering he only had a faded photo and Harry's own amateur sketch to work from. However, something else was bothering Harry. He had a secret, a secret never to be revealed and one that had burned inside him like a flame since he had met Elizabeth.

Peter

Peter had taken a chance when he was discharged from hospital many months after the war was over; it was his opportunity to change his previous sordid life. No happy childhood for him; he had been a troublesome, defiant child, disinterested in school, had no friends and despised convention. He had committed and been convicted of various minor crimes, mostly petty theft and shoplifting, any way to make a bob or two. Then the chance came to enlist in the forces; it appealed to Peter and gave his life a purpose, a reason to be part of something.

He had met Harry in Egypt; they had become inseparable and Peter knew all about Joanie and their love for each other. Peter had celebrated with Harry when he had received the telegram announcing the birth of his daughter, Elizabeth. He knew where the family lived and had also seen the locket in Harry's favourite photo of Joanie with baby Elizabeth.

When their unit was hit Harry had died instantly. Peter was devastated to see Harry's distorted body next to him and wept as he took the ID tag and the papers, letters and photos that Peter knew Harry carried with him at all times. But there followed another round of bombing and this time Peter didn't escape. He felt a searing pain in his legs and chest; then everything went black.

Maybe he hadn't intended to carry it through, maybe he just meant to find Elizabeth and give her Harry's property and tell her how brave her father had been? But the nurses and doctors had called him 'Harry' during his convalescence and, once his memory returned, he just didn't correct them. His search over the years for Elizabeth had been long and hard, interspersed with a variety of dead-end jobs to pay the rent on several seedy flats. But he had kept on the straight and narrow, not wanting to sully Harry's name, and then he had found her.

Elizabeth had been so eager to accept him as her father and never questioned him, it had been simple. After such a long time it would not be easy to admit that he wasn't the real Harry and, despite the fact that he had made Elizabeth happy, she would probably never forgive him for the deceit, and neither would Paula.

What was worse was that young Julie would be devastated if she lost her granddad.

Now the precious locket was lost. It had been the link between them and Harry felt that this had now been broken, just as his heart would be should it all end. His eyes filled with tears; he still had so much more to give but could he spend the rest of his days as an impostor? His head was spinning and he felt so very tired today. He couldn't go on living a lie. He would just have to confess and take the consequences. He removed the new locket from its velvet box and fingered it lovingly. He would give it to Elizabeth tonight and tell her and Max the truth.

Elizabeth

Elizabeth sat in the hospital canteen during her break, reflecting on her day. She was looking forward to finishing her shift and hurrying home to help Julie with her latest reading book.

Elizabeth liked her time on the medical ward at St Martin's, she got on well with the girls and they occasionally had evenings out at the nearby Angus Steak House for dinner and a bottle of Blue Nun. She liked being around the doctors and the banter with them. One of them had mentored her return to work. They had become close, very close, before his memory had started to fail him… Just as well, Elizabeth shivered; she had had too much to lose. That was in the past now.

For two half days a week, Elizabeth worked at the Blue Valley Day Centre. She liked being able to help the people who went there, even though most of them were away with the fairies! The majority of them were elderly, but not all, and it meant that she could keep an eye on the doctor who had helped her back into nursing, who was now himself in need of care. It was odd how things turn out.

Elizabeth glanced at the clock. Harry would be picking Julie up from school soon. She always preferred to call him Harry, and not 'Dad'. Elizabeth wondered if he noticed. She knew she could rely on him. Max was always busy and preoccupied with his job. Without Harry and Julie her home life would have been quite lonely.

Elizabeth was upset about the loss of her precious locket but she had something else on her mind, too. Harry and Paula were off to Australia in a month's time and she couldn't let Harry go before confronting him with what she had known for so long now; he was not her father. Oh, she had seen the papers, the medal and the photos but parts of his story just didn't add up. He had obviously known and respected her dad; he knew so much and her real dad must have liked and trusted this man, as indeed did she. Elizabeth and Max had accepted his story, always meaning to put an end to it when

'Harry' got on his feet. But they had lacked the courage, or was it just that they were scared that he would leave? They had grown to love him, he loved Julie and she adored having a granddad so it would have been terribly hard.

Elizabeth arrived home to see Harry playing Kerplunk with Julie, the two of them laughing and chatting together companionably. The deed had to be done, though; this difficult and heartbreaking situation could go on no longer. They all had dinner together and Harry took Julie up to bed for a story. Elizabeth looked at Max for reassurance. They had talked about it this morning and made their decision, Max nodded thoughtfully and sadly.

***

Harry limped up the stairs, followed by an insistent Julie.

"Can you tell me the Locket Story, Granddad? Oh, go on please," she implored. Unable to resist Julie's big, blue eyes, Harry nodded and when she was washed and tucked into bed Harry began.

"Once upon a time a young princess married a handsome prince, but he had to go on a long journey to distant lands. Before he went, he gave the princess a pretty blue locket, he told her it had magic powers and to wear it always. The magic must have worked because while he was away the princess gave birth to a beautiful baby girl with blue eyes that matched the locket. But the prince didn't come home from his travels and the princess was so sad that she died of a broken heart.

When the baby princess reached the age of ten she wore the locket just as her mother had done, near to her heart. She knew it was a magic locket and wished for a prince to come so that she wouldn't be lonely any more.

One day a dashing man arrived at the castle gates and after hearing the princess's story said he was her father. He had travelled far and wide; his ship had been taken by pirates and after a fierce storm the survivors became stranded on a deserted island and had to wait to be rescued. He hadn't known he had a daughter, he hadn't known he had lost his wife either, but something called to him to return home. The young princess believed his story and knew then that the locket had worked its magic."

Julie sighed sleepily.

"Thanks, Granddad, that is still the best story, do you think if they find it, Mummy will let me wear her locket when I'm older?"

Harry fingered the box in his pocket.

"Maybe, Julie, just maybe."

Norman's Conker

Lois Maulkin

He was pacing, pacing, measured steps and rather fast, as he was a little late. *Late for Sunday lunch*, he thought. *Or was it for piano practice? Did he play piano? Was it Sunday?* He wasn't sure, but he knew he was late, and he was pacing.

"Norman!" someone called from across the road. "Wait, Norman! Where are you going?"

He paused, and turned slowly, bare feet squeaking on the warm grass. "I'm going home," he said to Audrey Herring. Audrey Herring's blue rimmed spectacles flashed as she flicked her head from side to side at the kerb, readying to cross towards him with her blue rinse and blue leather shopping bag with one of the handles mended with tape. He knew the smell in that shopping bag, Chelsea bun round and used handkerchief. She stepped out into the sunshine and moved bulkily across the road, avoiding a Double Diamond lorry and a small boy on a Chopper.

"Don't come no nearer," he said.

"Don't be silly, Norman," said Audrey Herring, coming nearer. "What on earth are you doing out here? Where are your shoes?"

"I'm late, I've gone for a walk on the grass, and I've walked and walked. I think I'm late. Is it Sunday?"

"Wednesday, Norman. It's Wednesday. Early closing. Remember? We should be getting you back. Do you even know where you are?"

Norman looked about thoughtfully. Straight ahead, grass, stretching out for mile upon mile. Behind him, grass, green and trim, spreading back as far as he could see. "In the country," he said at last. "I'm collecting conkers."

"Blimey, Norman. You're not in the country, you're on the bypass. On the central reservation. It's really dangerous. Now, come on…" She grasped his hand and tucked it into the bend of her elbow. One finger caught on the handle of the shopping bag. "Let's be getting you home. Does Stella even know you're out? You run her ragged, you do, Norman. What with one thing and another all these years. That poor woman, what she's put up with and her with her shoes all worn through at the bunion. And talking of shoes, Norman, where are yours?" Audrey muttered to herself, and words including "conkers" and "bonkers" drifted out. The two of them moved on along the strip of green between the traffic.

He looked down at his feet, pacing steadily on below him, carrying him back the way he'd come across the miles and miles of grass. His feet had no idea where the old brown lace ups were, they just kept on walking, step after step after step. The ruined flick book of his memory had no idea where the shoes were.

"Think, Norman. Your shoes. Where are they?"

He thought. There was a red pullover with brown leather buttons, a silver heart with blue flowers on. And birdsong, and a forbidden garden, the smell of tomato plants sharp on Elizabeth's fingers. A box of Weekend chocolates. And at the side of a pebble-dashed house, where quince grew along the wooden lattice fence, the smell of creosote and Jeyes fluid. *Waggoner's Walk* floating from an open window. Elizabeth's shoes tossed into the grass. Shoes tapping down the path. Brown shoes. Brown shoes turning out of the gate. White dog turd. Missed it, thank heaven. Stella would be livid if he trod that all through the house again. Had he missed it? Maybe not. What if there was a bit caught at the bottom of his shoe, waiting to trap him, spread itself on the carpet? Stella's carpet. She did love him, he knew she did. But it was not the same now, not the same at all, not now, not since...

"I took them off to wipe them," he said, delighted to have pulled the memory out from somewhere.

"Where, Norman?" asked Audrey Herring, taking two Double Devon toffees out of a white paper bag in her pocket and handing him one. There was a little picture of a blue bird on the white wrapper, and he looked closely at it, smiling. He didn't answer Audrey Herring's question, because he couldn't, and he unwrapped the toffee and sucked it blankly.

Eventually, once they'd come off the bypass and walked back into the town and were stepping out briskly past the blinded shop fronts, they found the shoes balanced on the corner of a three sided bin advertising R Whites Lemonade.

"What's this inside?" asked Audrey Herring, picking something out of a shoe and holding it up between her thumb and forefinger. It swung in front of her face. She pursed her lips together.

"It's a conker, a little tiny conker on a string," said Norman, delighted. "I'll give it to Stella, she'll love it."

"Will she, now?" said Audrey Herring, in a voice that said she doubted it. She put down her shopping bag and bent to help Norman on with his shoes.

"She will," said Norman, absently gazing at a sign in the bakery window, telling him six slices a day was the well balanced way. "She'll love it, like Elizabeth did. She was looking and looking and looking for it."

Audrey Herring's head snapped round and she hissed "stop that now" at Norman. He was suddenly a little boy who'd dropped his milk at school, but then suddenly he wasn't, and he allowed Audrey Herring to march him along the High Road, and left into Castle

Street, and up to his front door, where she waved aside the flapping plastic ribbons of the fly screen and rapped on the pane with her knuckles. Stella answered the door, pulling a pale blue cardigan round herself and stood to one side as Audrey Herring and Norman swept in.

"Mrs Herring, come in," said Stella, "and Norman, I didn't even know you were out. Why aren't you asleep in front of *Crown Court*, like usual? Where've you been?"

"Out into the country, for conkers, and to bring you this." He passed across the gift, and Stella rubbed it gently with her thumb for a moment, before demanding, "Where did you get this?" Norman said, "Elizabeth gave it me."

"You're talking rubbish, Norman. It was in his shoe, Duck," said Audrey Herring quickly, "He left them somewhere and someone must have put it in. He's got a lot worse recently, hasn't he? I don't expect he makes much sense at all these days. Shall I put the kettle on?" She strode into the kitchen, taking off her coat as she went.

"What do you mean, in his shoe? It's a necklace, look."

"It's for you, Stella," said Norman. He looked into her face, and saw the girl she had once been looking back at him. He wanted to say something, something with meaning, something that would tell her how much he needed her and how the thought of losing her a tiny bit more every day, because he was losing himself, was an abyss of horror to him, but nothing would come and he sat down tiredly in the armchair facing the television. For a brief moment he saw again Elizabeth walking away. "We must forget everything," she'd said, and he had. He sank suddenly into sleep, as he was wont to do these last few years, just as Michael Barrett was preparing to take the country *Nationwide*.

Stella and Audrey Herring had a cup of tea and a pimply Lincoln biscuit, and Stella ran the necklace under the tap. It really was very pretty, and inside there were tiny photos of strangers smiling out happily at her. She laid it on the table next to the teapot. "I've always fancied myself in a locket, ever since that one on *Sale of the Century* back at Easter. It'll be worth nothing, of course. Not like that one Nicholas Parsons had. How funny to put something like this in a stranger's shoe. Whatever were they thinking? But it is lovely. Oh, Norman." She said. She had a few tears then, and dabbed her eyes with a small hanky.

***

Over the next year, Stella wore the locket often. Sometimes Norman smiled to see it on her, and briefly remembered Elizabeth again, just for a moment.

And on the final Wednesday afternoon, when the Stanwood's man had called to repair the television, and had all the valves out on a brown cloth on the carpet, and Stella came in to bring Norman and the Stanwood's man a cup of tea, she was wearing the locket, and it knocked on the side of Norman's face as she bent hurriedly over the armchair, in disbelief and a strangely resigned panic, to see if he was breathing still. And he wasn't breathing. He was just still.

Stella wore the locket to Norman's funeral. It had been the last gift he'd given her. She found she could not bring herself to take it off once he was gone. It was a link to him and she would pause, holding it in her hand, to remember the day he'd brought it home for her, and the look he'd given her, a look that made her think of people trapped and floating up under ice. She cried a lot, that first year.

In time, Stella sorted Norman's things and kept a box ready in the hall for the Boy Scouts' next jumble collection. And in time, when the Scouts knocked, she handed the box over – it held some cuff links and a red knitted pullover with leather buttons, some folded flannel shirts and a pencil case in the shape of a big red pencil – and unknown to her, the locket caught momentarily on the side of the box, and the chain pulled and the clasp slipped, and silently Norman's last present, Norman's conker, slid away into the box and back out of Stella's life.

A Flock of Seagulls

Lois Maulkin

Anyway, this particular summer's evening, we took the bus to the next town. I can't recall where we'd got this woman's number from, but I remember Theresa giggling behind me as we squashed into the phone box outside the Post Office and the smell of her Blasé perfume as I pushed in the ten pence piece and made an appointment for Friday evening.

We usually went to the pub on a Friday evening but fancied a change – this was just after all the pubs went pink. Do you remember that time? All the lovely old Windsor chairs and dartboards went onto skips and the pubs had their names chopped down and were refilled with pink and grey tub chairs and pink silk plants. I'd met Theresa in Den's (formerly The Queen of Denmark) one Friday night a couple of years back. We'd caught sight of each other in the grey smoked mirror tiles behind the bar and I'd done a double take as we were wearing matching lockets. "Snap!" she'd shouted, over Billy Idol's 'White Wedding'.

Luckily, it wasn't far from the bus stop to this woman's house. We'd had a couple of snakebites to fill the half hour before the bus was due, and I remember laughing as Theresa fell off the kerb at the corner of Blackbird Close, and then being outside the reeded glass front door of number six. Theresa said, "It's gone a bit dark – ever so spooooooky!" as she rang the bell, and I was choking in a giggle when the door was opened by this woman.

"Lovely," she said, standing back to let us in. She was short and middle-aged with hennaed hair to her shoulders and a lot less black eyeliner than we'd been somehow expecting. She wore jeans and a pink sweatshirt. "Yes. Lovely," she repeated, showing us into her living room.

"Right, ladies." she said, smiling pleasantly and shutting the door behind her. "If you don't mind, we'll start with business. My name's Marilyn. It's five pounds each for the reading, and I'll need a personal item from you for the psychometry. Something you wear a lot – a ring or a watch would be perfect. Obviously, that's just for me to hold for the duration." When she'd taken our money, she asked us to sit down and said she'd be back when she was ready for us.

***

We must have sat there for fifteen minutes. There were peach coloured swagged curtains and, in the corner, a television showing *The Tube* with the sound down. A copy of the *Radio Times* sat on the dark oak coffee table and a framed print of that man with his Suffolk Punches, ploughing through the watery light of a winter afternoon hung over the gas fire. Theresa and I spoke quietly to each other, and giggled, and I said I'd let Marilyn hold my locket for the reading. It had been mine for four years, and I wore it most days. My mum had given it to me, after I'd begged her for it, hideously. Though she liked it herself she hadn't worn it since she bought it at the Scouts' jumble sale years before so I didn't feel I was really depriving her of it.

And then Marilyn came back. And she'd changed. I don't mean she had on different clothes, she was dressed exactly the same, but there was something different about her, a feeling coming from her which hadn't come from her before, like a smell, but not a smell. She looked at us and said to me, "You first," and I told myself not to be ridiculous when I shivered as I stood up and followed her out of the room.

"Sit down, love," she said to me, as we went in to her dining room. The curtains were drawn closed, and we faced each other across an oval table. There was a dark cloth on the table and lighted candles in twisted ebony candlesticks to each side and we sat in a pool of faltering yellow light surrounded by inky shadow. A clock ticked slowly somewhere out of sight.

"I'll start with a prayer," she said, and I'm not religious but somehow, as she prayed for safety, I felt glad that she did. She took her tarot cards from a drawstring bag of purple velvet and smoothed them with her fingers – the word 'caress' came into my mind, and I heard it with a rolled 'r' in the middle, spoken slowly and wetly with a hiss at the end. "Cut these three times, please," she continued, handing the cards to me. They felt warm and thick and somehow gently fizzy to the touch. I cut them and passed them back. She drew a long breath and with one easy sweep of her hand spread them across the table into a long fan.

I can't remember the pictures. She laid the cards out in different patterns, talking all the time in a low voice, steadily, telling me things I knew and things I didn't. I'd expected her to ask questions, to gather clues to whip into a froth she could present as new information, but she didn't, and some of the things she said to me made me wonder if Theresa had spoken to her separately, and told her about my childhood and my hopes.

And then she asked for my locket. She held it in one hand and looked at me for what seemed like a really long time, and I realised I couldn't hear the clock ticking – it was as though it was holding its breath – and then she said to me, "There is a lot of sadness here." I had the feeling she was choosing her words particularly carefully. She asked if I knew the locket's history and I shook my head, suddenly feeling the back of my neck prickle. And then she sat back in the chair, and I'm not making this up, I swear, the room went icy cold, and she closed her eyes and took a big, shuddery breath, paused for what seemed like ages, and hissed the word 'Joanie', which isn't my name but which scared the life out of me. I wanted to jump up and run out, but I couldn't move. It was like being in a dream where you're trapped in a sea of jelly, and your heart is banging like a chop bone in the waste disposal. I made a bit of a whimpering sound, and she knocked on the table with the flat of her hand and said sternly, "Sit quiet and listen. You must take care. Ill fortune follows this like seagulls follow the plough. Sorrow, sorrow and deceit, and, and worse." With that, she dropped the locket quickly onto the table and rubbed her hand, and I could see a red welt coming up in her palm.

"Oh my goodness," she said, and gave a little laugh as though pulling herself together. "Well, that was dramatic, wasn't it? I am sorry. I do try not to scare people but sometimes it all gets a bit much." I stood up hurriedly and stumbled out. She was still rubbing her hand as she followed me into the living room and said, "Ready, Theresa?"

Theresa went out, and I sat down on the settee and took some deep breaths. I found myself looking at the picture over the fireplace, with the ploughman striding out in the rough brown furrows of his antique trousers, and I saw there were seagulls all around him and realised I hadn't noticed them before. To stop myself looking and thinking about seagulls following I picked up the *Radio Times*, but before I could open it, Theresa was back. She said, "Come on," and we left, with Marilyn standing in the hall, silently opening the front door and closing it slowly behind us once we'd stepped out into the dusk.

"What did she say to you?" I asked as we stood at the bus stop.

"Nothing," said Theresa. "Well, next to nothing. She spread out the cards and had a quick look then came over all brisk and said she was sorry but she couldn't read anything for me, and gave me my money back. So, of course," she waggled her eyebrows comically, "that means snakebites!" Theresa waved her five pound note in front of my face and then she looked and asked why I wasn't wearing my locket, and I told her what had happened.

"Absolute rubbish," she announced. "Tell me you don't think there's anything in it all, please!" and I couldn't answer, because I really wasn't sure why but I really didn't want to put the locket on.

"So, what, you're never going to wear it again?" Theresa said after a while. "That's silly. Tell you what, let's swap." She pulled my silver heart out of my jacket pocket, and slipped the chain over her head. She took hers off and tried to put it over my head, but I said, "Stop it, Theresa," turning away from her quickly. She laughed and kind of stumbled off the kerb, and this is the silly part, the bus was just suddenly there, and

Theresa was a shaking red flower under the wheel and spread out and melting across the road, and there was this screaming and screaming and it was coming from me.

***

Theresa was buried wearing her locket, and her mother sent mine back to me in a very kind letter, but I never wore it again. I was a different person after all that happened.

    I went back to see Marilyn once or twice – I suppose I was hoping to sponge away my guilt with that warm soapy idea of nothing being foreshadowed. But one time I went in and the air was suddenly filled with the scent of Blasé, and I felt I was choking and ran out and never went back. I kept the locket wrapped in a black sock in a shoe box under the stairs, and was half relieved and half horrified when I found out some years later that it had been accidentally taken to the Oxfam shop. I am tired these days. I don't sleep well. My nights are full of dreams of seagulls.

Blue

Sue Duggans

Jennifer stumbled into the charity shop almost by accident. A sudden, torrential downpour had left shoppers dashing for cover in all directions.

It was the vivid blue of the flowers that caught her eye. As she fumbled through assorted bric-a-brac there it was. Her fingers, still wet from the rain, picked the locket from the chipped dish. She held it in her moist palm and stared long and hard at the charming, heart-shaped piece. It was the blue. Her mind and her heart (shattered by Geoff's sudden departure) raced to the ocean and her beloved son. Jennifer felt the sadness of his absence wash over her unexpectedly. Her eyes pricked and she was relieved that the raindrops, still trickling down her forehead and cheeks, disguised her unexpected tears.

Geoff, his name hugely influenced by his father's love of football, was born in 1966, the first and only child of Jennifer and Ken. When she held her baby son in her arms, Jennifer noticed how his blue eyes shone, as if lit from within. As he grew and flourished, his eyes sparkled, reflecting his spirit.

"Hi, Jen." The familiar, welcome voice of Jennifer's close friend, Sally, brought her back to the reality of 1995. "Deep in thought?" she continued.

"Yep! Could say that," Jennifer replied, relieved to have her wayward thoughts back in the here and now.

"Found anything worth buying?" Sally enquired, glancing at the chain dangling from Jennifer's clenched fist.

"I like the look of this," came her measured reply, attempting to play down the impact of this small, well-crafted piece of jewellery. Jennifer paid the smiling cashier.

"What a pretty locket!" She sounded genuine. Jennifer slipped it into the pocket of her sodden jacket and the two friends left.

The rain had eased. Jennifer and Sally strolled along, comfortable in each other's company. They chose a small, cramped coffee shop near the station. The women ordered hot chocolate and manoeuvred themselves into chairs at a table overlooking the currently out-of-use patio area. Autumn leaves swirled and danced in the corner, trying to entertain on a dismal afternoon. The leaden sky threatened more rain.

Good friends, like hot chocolate, are comforting and the two sipped in silence, warming their chilled hands on ample mugs.

Sally broke the silence. "You seemed far away when I first spotted you."

"Mmm. Geoff's been gone for seven months now and I miss him so much." Jennifer paused, before adding, "He's been offered a permanent contract in New York."

"Save up your pennies and visit him." Sally's response seemed almost flippant and Jennifer experienced a fleeting sense of intense loss.

***

Life for Jennifer and Ken bumbled on through late autumn, peppered with occasional social events. They booked a weekend with Sally and Rob in London at the beginning of December. Ken and Rob had worked together for several years in the eighties and, like their wives, were at ease with each other.

The magic of Christmas was etched on the faces of small children gazing at window displays in West End stores. The twinkle of lights, strains of familiar carols and Santa himself (reindeer and elves conveniently parked 'round the back', out of view) left no doubt about the time of year.

The group enjoyed a wonderful evening meal in the hotel restaurant. Conversation flowed easily, as did the wine. Rob pulled himself to his feet and raised his glass.

"A toast to absent friends!" He spoke the words with vigour then dropped noiselessly to his seat.

Pause. Jennifer was feeling emotional and quietly urged herself to be rational. Rob and Ken had spent the last hour or so reminiscing about the old days in the Norwich office. Clearly there was no hidden agenda in his toast. How would she smile on Christmas morning with her beloved son so far away? She could feel her spirits sinking fast, aided by generous quantities of wine. She said her 'good nights' and took herself to bed. When Ken joined her some time later, he climbed into bed quietly so as not to wake his sleeping wife. He was unaware of Jennifer's tearstained pillow.

By morning, Jennifer's heavy spirit had lifted. The couples took a leisurely stroll through St James's Park. Jennifer and Sally chatted about catering arrangements for Christmas whilst the men talked sport, the fortunes of Ken's beloved West Ham United and the prospect of a holiday in France for the World Cup in 1998. The sun shone and warmed the bracing air. Before travelling back, the quartet lunched in a small Italian restaurant near Covent Garden and plans were made for Christmas evening at Jennifer and Ken's.

***

Christmas morning arrived. Jennifer was an organised, tidy-minded woman and preparations had been made well in advance. The house, which had been their family home for twenty-seven years, gleamed. The first

Christmas there had been different. Having just moved in, there were unpacked boxes stacked neatly behind the tree. The house was drab but alight with the presence of their adored son, his chatter and squeals of excitement filling their hearts with joy.

Ken seemed slightly uneasy as he busied himself preparing the table for lunch. It would be a quiet affair – Jennifer, Ken and his widowed brother Paul. He shuffled place mats from here to there and seemed preoccupied as he polished the cutlery. Jennifer caught a glimpse of him; tall, slim, his silver hair evidence of the passing years, handsome. However, his uncharacteristic abandonment of calm bothered her.

When cooking was underway and the house filled with the various aromas of Christmas lunch, Jennifer slipped upstairs to change. On the way up she caught sight of Ken on the phone in the lounge in hushed conversation. She paused momentarily. Several minutes later, dressed and ready for the occasion in her new pastel blue dress, she reached for her locket which was laid in readiness on the dressing table. As she fumbled to fix the clasp, the doorbell rang. Her ears pricked. She was aware of Ken answering the door and heard him gasp. Silence. She raced to the top of the stairs and her heart leapt.

There he was; Geoff returned. Never before had she descended the stairs at such speed. She threw her arms around her Christmas surprise!

"Hi, Mum. Happy Christmas!" Jennifer's heart pounded and her eyes filled with tears. She glanced through wet lashes at Ken and knew, in an instant, that this had been his well-kept secret.

In her excitement, Jennifer's usual good manners had momentarily deserted her. She stepped back and, with glistening eyes and a warm smile, welcomed the pretty, slim young girl standing by Geoff.

"Mum, this is Julie." The two women embraced in warm informality. Geoff had spoken about his close friendship with an English girl who worked in the New York office.

Paul arrived within moments. "I managed to park round the corner," he announced. There was a spring in his step and a twinkle in his eye which had been absent for some time. Paul and his wife, Maggie, had been childless and they loved Geoff like their own son.

"Uncle Paul collected us from the airport yesterday and we stayed with him overnight," Geoff explained.

"You rascal, Paul!" Jennifer exclaimed. "Now I know why you turned down our offer of a bed last night."

"And you!" She turned to Ken, wagging her finger at him in playful admonishment, and put her arms around him, hugging him tightly. Through the mist she could see him smile lovingly at her.

Jennifer moved reluctantly into the kitchen to slow the cooking and Ken quickly shifted table settings and laid two additional places.

Over drinks, Jennifer learned that Geoff had met Julie during his first weekend in America. Julie confessed that she had disappointed her mother by not following her into a nursing career. Instead she trained in accountancy and was nine months into a two year internship at the World Trade Centre offices where Geoff worked.

Since meeting, the couple had become 'an item' and spent most weekends exploring the spectacular sights of New York State. Their most recent travels took them north to Niagara and they had booked a short break skiing at Lake Placid in February. By remarkable coincidence Julie's family lived only thirty miles away from Jennifer and Ken and the couple would be travelling to see them on the 29th before flying back to New York on New Year's Day.

Lunch was a wonderful feast and the five ate and chatted alternately. Jennifer sat opposite her son and his delightful girlfriend who both radiated contentment.

Whilst the men cleared the table, Julie helped Jennifer make coffee.

"I noticed your locket. It's sweet, very pretty." Julie spoke and then paused.

Jennifer responded casually, "I picked it up in a charity shop just recently. It had instant appeal."

Julie was quiet as she busied herself arranging the tray; gold-wrapped mints laid out so precisely and china cups, handles facing due east, were arranged meticulously. That heart-shaped locket with vivid blue flowers was preoccupying her thoughts, she was sure that it was the same one her mother wore all the time when Julie was a child and then it had been lost. Her mother, Elizabeth, had given her a replica to wear but it lacked the charm and craftsmanship of the original piece and Julie had eventually swapped it with her school friend, Theresa, for a butterfly clip and a lip gloss.

Millennium Bug

Josephine Gibson

12.45 a.m. 1 January 2000: London

Geoff sighed and leaning back in his chair, stretched his arms in the air.

It had been a long night. The TV was still chattering in the corner, the table was strewn with cake boxes, crisp crumbs were all over the floor. He stood up and walked to the water dispenser, filled a cup and took a long drink while surveying the rest of the office through the glass partition of the meeting room. A few of the guys had returned to their desks and were idly chatting to each other. There was none of the usual frantic activity; no one was looking at the clocks that told them the time in New York, London and Tokyo. The banks of computer screens were blank now, mission control was closing down.

Geoff tutted to himself. The 'millennium bug'. More like a millennium damp squib. He raised his eyebrows, thinking about the computer programmers of the sixties and seventies. Although he owed his career to computing, those early programmers had left a legacy for which he'd become responsible. He had led the team that spent months preparing for the bug, Y2K, ensuring that none of the bank's computers would be affected. Despite his certainty that they had covered all eventualities, they'd all been called in to spend New Year's Eve watching the systems to check billions of dollars were not about to be wiped out.

Frankly, he would much have preferred to have spent New Year's Eve with his growing family rather than sitting here with his colleagues, eating supermarket treat sized cakes and watching the great and good enjoy a party at the Millennium Dome. It had been amusing to see the Queen's reaction to being invited to sing Auld Lang Syne by Tony Blair, but that was a small moment in a frustrating night of boredom. Although he would probably have lost his job if the millennium bug had affected the systems, there was a part of him that would have relished some action at midnight and a chance to prove to Julie that their enforced separation was worth it.

"Oh, Geoff," she had said, sadly, when he told her. She said no more but dropped her eyes to the cup of tea she was holding, her only sign of distress a tightening of her fingers around the rim. He would have preferred a stronger reaction so that he could shout, bluster, justify, but instead he felt a lonely gulf of guilt between them.

He sighed again and moved to the window, looking out across the many lit windows of City skyscrapers. They reminded him somewhat of Tetris; there were irregular rectangular blocks of light and darkness, both horizontal and vertical – depending, presumably, on the function of the office within. He was aware that all over the City teams like his were at work.

In the past he had found it invigorating, exciting even, to be a part of the greatest financial centre in the world. But now, somehow, the joy of using his brain and his skills had faded. He had begun to resent his work, his daily commute, the young arrogant men who threw their weight around, thinking they ruled the world with their Essex accents, their cufflinks and their Rolex watches. It was a world where the traders ruled, where their demands had to be met, despite many patient explanations of the complexities of computer systems. Geoff continued to smile, shake hands, defer and endure; all so that he could earn a living and provide for his family. Yet it all seemed so pointless when he worked such long hours that he hardly saw them.

He thought of his little boys who would be fast asleep, their faces flushed with the warmth of their duvets, their golden curls on the pillow. He loved to see them like this; dreaming, peaceful, not confused by their mother's withdrawal when they called on her for attention.

"They're only babies," he murmured, leaning his forehead on the cool dark glass of window overlooking the City. Beautiful boys who deserved the best. He took a deep breath – time to go home to them.

***

12.45 a.m. 1 January 2000: Surrey

"1, 2, 3, 4, 5, 6
No.
1, 2, 3, 4, 5, 6
Ugh!
1, 2, 3, 4, 5, 6
7, 8, 9, 10, 11, 12
Ah, that's it."

Julie was counting kitchen cupboard fronts. They needed to be counted in the right order – first, the row across the top. *Then,* the ones along the bottom. They had to be cleaned in that order too. If she got it wrong she'd have to start again. She only had two more to go. Please God she didn't make a mistake, it was so late and she was so tired.

First, the handle. This was vital. It was touched by anyone who used the cupboard. She scrubbed at the base of the handle – where dirt could stick – with a small brush she had dipped into disinfectant. She wiped the drips away with a piece of kitchen roll that she immediately disposed of in a small bin bag next to where she was kneeling.

She moved on to the cupboard front. She didn't want to finish the handle until she had thoroughly cleaned the door, because she needed to touch the handle to open it and wipe around the edges. She resolutely turned from the thought of cleaning the inside of the doors. It would be all right. It would be all right. She didn't need to clean them now.

But would it? Oh God! No, no, it would. Calm down.

"Cupboard locks. Cupboard locks. It's OK. Cupboard locks."

The boys couldn't open the doors. Geoff had toddler proofed the kitchen. But what if they touched the inside of the door when she opened it? Perhaps she had better clean the insides of the bottom six. Should she go back and start again? Would it be better to go back to the start, or should she finish the last two, and clean the insides on them, then go back to the first four?

But if she did that, she would finish at number 10, not number 12.

"Ugh!"

"Perhaps I could leave the insides?"

But if she did, if she cut corners, it wouldn't be right. She wouldn't sleep, anyway, knowing it was wrong. No, the only thing to do was finish cleaning 11 and 12, on the outside, then start again at number 6, cleaning them all properly, insides and outsides because she'd be touching the outsides so they'd be dirty. Numbers 6 to

12, it was the only way. It never worked to try and save time.

And so Julie knelt, wiping, scrubbing, counting, thinking, with distant music and the occasional firework to accompany her, until Geoff came in at 3.00 a.m. and gently picked her up and held her, stroking her hair, telling her it was OK, he was home, the boys were safe, and she could sleep now.

***

12.45 p.m. 1 January 2000: Essex

Jennifer looked out of the window again, peering along the road to see if there was any sign of Geoff's 4x4. She was so excited to think of the twins. She had everything ready for them. Their beds were made and a selection of soft toys was sitting on the pillows. Ken had spent the morning wrapping presents and arranging them around the Christmas tree, which she had insisted on keeping up, because she had wanted to spend Christmas with her grandsons. It was so disappointing that Geoff and Julie had said they wanted a quiet family Christmas. Surely she and Ken were family? It wasn't as if they expected to be entertained, she'd cooked dozens of Christmas dinners and would have happily taken over and let Julie rest and play with the children while she cooked.

She smiled to herself. Yes, taking over, that was probably the problem. A relationship with a daughter-in-law felt like a very intricate dance. Maybe it was the equivalent of those Scottish dances where men jump over crossed swords. A wrong move and you'd slice your foot open. She didn't want to risk her relationship with Geoff and the boys by being a bossy mother-in-law and pushing Julie away.

She still wished Julie would let her help. It was obvious she was struggling since the twins had been born. She always looked so tired and sat quietly, not joining the conversation, not paying attention to the twins, letting Ken amuse them without the trace of a smile when they laughed at their silly grandfather's face.

Never mind. As long as Geoff was happy, it wasn't for her to judge. She glanced around the room nervously. She supposed Julie must think her very boring and suburban; she and Ken had lived in their semi for most of their married life, they still had some of Geoff's toys in the loft, waiting for the boys to be old enough to play with them.

It was such a shame they lived on the other side of London! What was wrong with Essex? It would be much more convenient for Geoff's commuting than Surrey. She'd have more of an opportunity to look after the boys if they lived closer. It was a crying shame she couldn't see more of her grandsons.

No, she was doing it again. She must not complain. She had to smile, be welcoming, try and be cheerful. For Geoff's sake. For the boys' sake. For her own sake. She felt a cold trickle of fear in her chest as she imagined Geoff and Julie splitting up. What would Julie do then? Would she and Ken be welcomed if they wanted to visit their grandsons?

No, this wouldn't do. She mustn't think like this. She fingered the locket hanging on a silver chain around her neck. She was going to give it to Julie today. She had always seemed to admire it, covet it even, and although Jennifer loved it for the memories of Geoff it gave her, it was after all only a trinket. Nothing was as important as keeping the family together. She rehearsed her little speech to Julie, to be given after the boys had opened their presents:

"Dearest Julie, Ken and I would love to be able to treat you to a lovely piece of jewellery, but you know we are just a couple of old pensioners without a clue about what is fashionable. So I thought I'd pass on my locket to you – I don't have any daughters of my own so I would love you to have it as my daughter-in-law. We are so happy to have you in our family and for you to have given us our lovely grandsons."

***

3.45 p.m. 1 January 2000: Essex

Jennifer filled the kettle with water, blinking to clear her eyes. She could feel a lump in her throat and she sniffed, determined not to cry. She heard Ken come into the room, place the tray of cups and saucers down on the table, then come over to her. He placed a hand on her shoulder.

"Well, can you believe it? What are the chances of that? Your locket belonging to Julie's mother and grandmother! I wouldn't have believed it myself, if she hadn't had that photo in her purse. You can tell it's the same person as the one in the locket. Unbelievable! Remind me, where did you get it?"

"Mum," Geoff had followed his father into the room. "I just need to refill the twins' drinks. They seem thirsty today, I wonder if..."

Jennifer and Ken weren't able to hear the rest of his sentence because it was interrupted by Julie's low, heartfelt scream from the sitting room:

"Nooooo! Nooooo! It's dirty, it's dirty! Don't touch it!"

There was a crash and a wailing from one of the twins, followed quickly by his brother crying in sympathy. The three adults rushed back into the room. Julie had collapsed sobbing on the floor, her head bowed against her knees, her arms crossed around her shins. Two confused little boys stood near her, dry eyed but noisy, keening in tandem. The locket, which Jennifer a moment before had placed on the occasional table before offering to make more tea, lay across the room, split in half at the hinge.

Geoff stared at the shocked face of his mother, at Julie's muffled sobbing, at his dad moving to comfort the twins with a hug, and at the broken locket on the floor. He sank on the sofa next to Julie, ineffectively rubbing her back. The tiredness he had been holding at bay all day filled his mind, making him feel lightheaded and a memory of the City's lights of the night before came back to him. He realised the months spent on the millennium bug, of trying to right the wrongs of the past, had been wasted. It was here, in his family, that the virus existed.

For Julie, the light was shattering into pieces. The bombs dropping out of a clear, blue, Egyptian sky; the grandmother losing hope on a pale winter afternoon; her mother's obscured view of her roots – all became focused in a moment, the sun shining through the magnifying glass of the locket – setting Julie alight with her fear for her sons; so that all she could do was smash the locket and let the comfort of darkness take over.

Laurie, the famous actress (protagonist)

To save mother (goal)

Irene, the temptress (obstacle)

Gets on television (action)

Double Trouble

Sue Duggans

She stood there, poised, flanked by her two weird sisters. Their hearts were beating faster than usual, pulsating in their necks and sweat beads were gathering on their brows. They were anticipating the crash and when it came they knew this was it. Flashes of lightning, more thunder crashes and the curtain rose.

It was the first night of the Royal Shakespeare Company's latest production of *Macbeth*. The theatre was packed and the first scene, with its spectacular technologies, brought with it an air of exhilaration.

'When shall we three meet again
In thunder, lightning, or in rain?'

Lorraine the famous actress, known as Laurie to her close friends and family, felt a rush of adrenaline as she spoke her first words. This was her debut stage role after years of working in television and films. By the time the cauldron scene and celebrated witches' chant was underway, first night nerves had evaporated into the dark air unlike the dark air still hanging in Laurie's heart.

'In the poisoned entrails throw.'

Through the spiders which were her eyelashes, the famous actress became aware of Lady Macbeth standing in the wing bathed in green light. The green of her stunning gown momentarily caught her eye. Her twin sister Irene (older by some fifteen minutes) had won the leading role which Laurie believed without doubt would be hers. Damn her! Irene, who hadn't even gone to Drama College and slogged for three years but dabbled in a two year foundation course and got some experience in local amateur dramatics. Then the shocking business with mother!

'Double, double toil and trouble,
Fire burn and cauldron bubble.'

The irony of her twin sister's role had been something that Laurie mused upon over and over again. The temptress Lady Macbeth, the devilish wife of Macbeth, whose ambition drove her husband to the desperate act of murder! It hadn't been thoughts of murder in Irene's heart but greed and it was her unforgivable treachery which led to the twins' bond being severed, like the umbilical cord at birth, for ever.

It was by chance that Laurie discovered the awful truth of her sister's deception. 'Lady Macbeth', it transpired, had been attempting to coerce their mother into selling her cherished family home, stopping at nothing to get her hands on the spoils of the sale. Although frail and vulnerable, the twins' mother still had all her faculties and it became Laurie's mission to save her from her sister's fraudulent and devious plan.

After months of legal wrangling and vitriolic dispute, Irene stood before the judge, her head bent slightly. She was lucky to get away with a period of probation and not a custodial sentence.

After the court case Laurie sent her twin a card. She wrote inside 'Fraud is the daughter of greed.' Nothing more. However, there was no doubt Irene would have identified the author.

'Double, double toil and trouble;
Fire burn and cauldron bubble.'

Laurie listened intently to her witch sisters as they cackled out their lines and she smiled wryly as she heard the words 'Witches' Mummy'. She reversed them again and again in her head, *Mummy's witch, Mummy's witch, Mummy's witch.* Then once more the chant in unison:

'*Double, double toil and trouble;*
Fire burn and cauldron bubble.'

The green figure was no longer in the wing.

The after-party was a subdued affair, being the first night of many, but excitement rose when the director announced the lead players for the next production – *Romeo and Juliet*. Laurie was delighted, and only a little surprised, when she was awarded Juliet. Whilst being heartily congratulated by the cast, she noticed Irene. Her face was stony and Laurie detected an anxiety in her twin. Was it the result of Laurie's part as the next Juliet, a jewel amongst Shakespearian roles? Or might it be that, like Lady Macbeth, her guilt was sending her into madness?

Saving Mother

Barbara Sleap

Laurie sighed heavily as she sank into the battered chair in her dressing room. Another performance over, only two more months to go. It was becoming a bit too much now, she was nearly sixty and envied other women of her age relaxing in spas, having long lunches with friends and making shopping trips. Here she was though, trying to juggle her life between the theatre, and looking after her elderly and slightly senile mother who lived on her own nearby. Her younger sister, *Irene*, didn't help. She was always gallivanting around with some man or other; she met them on an internet dating site and called herself '*The Temptress*' which just about said it all.

Laurie had *saved her mother* several times now and in the last month she had discovered her wandering around the local Tesco Superstore, found her eating a lunch of raw bacon sandwiches and yesterday she had arrived to find the kitchen floor flooded while her mother slept obliviously in the bedroom. Something drastic had to be done before a serious accident happened. Laurie had suggested to Irene that they find a nice care home for their mother, in fact Laurie had been to see a couple and there was one in particular that would have been perfect. Irene, however, said it would be too expensive and would use up too much of Mum's money. Laurie knew that Irene was only interested in their inheritance which was mostly tied up in their Mother's luxury bungalow which was now sadly deteriorating.

Laurie had an idea though and knowing how Irene fell for, and trusted, the most unsuitable men, she decided that now was the time to take action. To do this she had to engage the help of her theatre friends and one in particular; the debonair, smooth talking Victor Le Doyen (whose real name was Henry Gregson). Victor always took the part of a glib womaniser and in his earlier days had been a minor heartthrob. Laurie was aware of his reputation with women, both young and old, but Victor didn't care what people thought. Laurie decided to arrange a small soiree at home one Sunday evening and invited Irene who had been delighted to accept. Laurie usually tended to keep her sister well away from her thespian friends.

The evening started quietly and the small room gradually filled with the actresses and actors that Laurie was closest to. Irene arrived in a stunning, emerald green silk, skimpy dress; it was tight and short with a plunging neckline which left nothing to the imagination. Her newly-coloured red hair was swept up high on her head and she greeted everyone coyly from beneath thick black false eyelashes. Laurie looked over at Victor who was eyeing Irene lustily – her little ruse seemed to be working. She had confided her worries about her mother to Victor who had oozed sympathy and had agreed with all of her suggestions to save her mum. Laurie hoped that as Irene would not listen to her, she might take notice of Victor.

Irene looked around the room and tottered straight over to where Victor was standing, he in turn left the couple he had been chatting to and greeted Irene with a gushing kiss. Irene giggled and fluttered her eyelashes like a lovesick teenager.

The evening went well; Victor had been overly attentive to Irene the whole evening and as Laurie looked over she saw them deep in conversation. Victor had his arm resting loosely around Irene's waist and Laurie surprised herself by thinking what a handsome couple they made. Gradually everyone drifted away and, as he left, Victor gave Laurie a knowing wink and kissed Irene's hand flamboyantly. She giggled and blushed in response.

The next few weeks for Laurie were a hectic round of performances and sorting out her mother as best as her time allowed. She had hardly seen Irene and was disappointed that she hadn't contacted her after the party. She hadn't seen much of Victor either, outside of their stage relationship. Mother seemed to be getting worse; she was very forgetful and sometimes got angry with Laurie when she tried to help her. It was all very worrying and she was even more determined to resolve the dilemma somehow.

At last, the play had finished and Laurie looked forward to a relaxing summer. She had reluctantly turned down a fairly decent part in a drama set in New York but she knew that she couldn't leave her mother for what would probably be a few months. The day after the end of show party, Laurie opened the door to Irene who entered flourishing a bottle of Cava. Laurie was immediately suspicious but popped the bottle and sat opposite her sister, giving her a questioning look.

"I'm getting married," blurted Irene, blushing as she did so.

"To who?" Laurie asked in a shocked voice.

"Well, to Victor, of course, you must have guessed."

Laurie stared at her sister; it was unbelievable. Irene had already had one disastrous marriage and had vowed she would never venture down that path again.

Laurie stuttered, "B... b... but you can't be serious darling, he's a womaniser and has done this before, believe me."

"We're crazy about each other, Laurie, he said it's different this time and once we're married we're going to spend the winter in France."

"Well what about me and Mum? What am I supposed to do while you're living it up on the Riviera?"

"Oh, Victor and I have discussed this and we think it's best if you do as you've suggested and put her in a home. You can get the bungalow decorated and rent it out, that should help cover the care fees. In fact, we've been to see Mum a couple of times and she was quite happy about it, she really liked Victor and said he reminded her of Dad."

Laurie spluttered into her glass, "My, you've certainly been busy, the pair of you, I bet Mum doesn't even remember your visit." She sat up tall in the chair. "Well, actually you've both done me a favour, as you seem to have it all sorted out, I can take the TV part I've been offered in New York, you know I've always wanted to make *it on television*. I had turned it down but now Mum's taken care of I'll be able to go. It'll only be for about three months and I can pop back for the wedding. Actually, I'm surprised Victor didn't accept the part he was offered, absolutely perfect for him, an errant husband who is murdered by his long suffering wife, absolutely perfect."

Irene shifted uncomfortably and took a long slurp of Cava. "But you can't leave it all to us," she said tearfully, "it's not fair."

"Not fair! Not fair!" Laurie half shouted, "I've done everything for the last five years while you've been swanning about with man after man. Well, now it's your turn. Oh, and by the way, did you know Victor can't even speak French?" She leant back and studied her sister's broken expression.

"We're having lessons," Irene said, staring soulfully into her glass, which was now empty. She reached over and refilled it.

Laurie stood up and went to the sideboard drawer. She returned to the table with a pile of leaflets.

"I'll give you these now, darling, so that you can put things in motion straight away. This one has the details of the care home…it's lovely, right on the seafront, Mum will love it…these are details of a letting agent, I spoke to a girl called Sharon some time ago and here are some quotes I had done for redecorations on the bungalow but they're probably out of date now."

Laurie fetched her handbag, pulled out her chequebook, scribbled an amount and handed the cheque to Irene. "This is a wedding present; £500. I think that's quite generous don't you? Just one tip though, don't let Victor get hold of it, you do know he's a bit of a gambler don't you?"

Laurie noticed the flicker pass across her sister's face, "Well, I really must be getting on darling, I've got a million phone calls to make, you can see yourself out can't you, I'm really grateful to you and Victor, such a relief, oh and thanks for the fizzy." With that Laurie stalked majestically from the room.

On the way up to her office Laurie pondered on her sister's visit. "It seems that I have succeeded in saving Mum, but I think I might soon have to save my sister as well."

The Ripper

Lois Maulkin

I saw her the other day. Thursday, it was. She was coming out of Primark with a great big bag of stuff. She cuts out the labels, you know, and sews in posher ones she nicks from the clothes in charity shops. They call her 'The Ripper' in Homes for the Helpless. The manager has to follow her round and make conversation with her, really close, like, so she doesn't get a chance to get her scissors out. Mind you, that's sometimes worse, because if she can't cut out the labels she just tears them. And, of course, they don't come out that easily. There aren't many designer clothes that fetch much with big chunks torn out of them and the necks all stretched and frayed. Well, apart from early Vivienne Westwood, I suppose.

Anyway, as I was saying, that Thursday, she had her sunglasses on and her collar turned up but I'd know her anywhere. I went up to her and said, "Hello Mum," and she looked right through me. Stunk of gin, she did. I felt quite jealous. "Been on a spree?" I asked, nodding towards her bag, but she just kind of bustled away. I went after her, of course, and got in front of her, and said "Mum, I haven't seen you since, well, since Dad had that fling with Irene – can we go for a drink and catch up, maybe?"

She hissed at me, really, she did, she hissed, it's the only word to use. She told me to bugger off, and I was hurt, frankly. And then she stamped on my foot and shot into the bus station. And she never gets the bus, at least, not when it's busy like it was that day, and never the number nineteen; that goes right up by the gas works and she won't be seen dead up there, not since that episode with Irene's husband when he came to read her meter and she kept him prisoner under the stairs for a week.

I kept as near to her as I could, but she moves quickly, does Mum, when she's a mind to, and before you could say 'knife' she was tucked into the crowd waiting for the blessed number nineteen. And then there was a kind of fuss following her. The bus queues rippled and a few people tottered out of line and two massive great blokes in navy blue suits with huge necks and curly black wires going into their ears barged up to her and seized her by the arms.

My God, I thought, *she's been on the rob again*, and I fluffed out my hair and strode up, smiling brightly, like I do on that ad for cooking oil when my chips are voted the shiniest, and I said, "Excuse me, gentlemen, there must be some mistake. Now, I know what you're thinking. You're thinking I look just like Laurie Luton, aren't you? Well, I am Laurie Luton, and this is my mother. Sometimes she's a little, erm, absent minded. Perhaps she's left the store without paying for absolutely everything? Please allow me to settle up any outstanding amount. And perhaps I could give you gentlemen an autographed picture of myself by way of thanks for being so understanding? Perhaps with my phone number on?"

I always carry a few headshots with me for just such eventualities. I opened my bag and fished a couple out. We were quite the focus of attention by now, and while Mum was wriggling and swearing and stinking of booze, I was in professional mode, you know how I do it, *very* sweet, *very*, well, the only word I can think of to use and I know it probably makes me sound big headed, but really *very beautiful* is the only way to describe me then. When I'm at my best. With an audience. You know. And I had them. Those big, burly, brutes of men, they were like putty in my hands, and I knew it would all be all right, when, like a fork down a blackboard, up pipes a voice: "She's got half the household linen department down the front of her frock," and it was that damned trollop Irene, smirking, she was, with her greasy red lips sliding about all over her face and her cleavage sagging out like going down balloons the week after the carnival's been through.

I didn't lose it. I was charm itself and I just gave that tinkling laugh, the famous one that says I know how to suck blancmange from a widow's slipper (perhaps that's not quite so famous after all, come to think of it, at least I've never seen Widow's Slipper in Tesco since, anyway), and started writing my phone number on one of the photos, and said, "Oh, Irene, you are a card. Here, gentlemen, my personal number. My friend's just having a little joke, and I'm sure we've no need for unpleasantness. Shall we go back to the shop so I can sort out any oversight?"

And then the number nineteen pulled up at the stop, and Irene's husband was on it, with his meter reader's cap on, and Mum saw him. And it seemed to trigger something in her. A shudder rippled through her, her eyes went all wide and she let out an inhuman howl, like a ghost that's shut its thumb in a drawer. And all the hair on the back of my neck bristled out in a way that would have had me thrown off those SlickFatAntiStat Conditioner ads, and no word of a lie, my bun unwound itself and my foam doughnut fell off the back of my head. And that Irene, she laughed and laughed, ever so hard and then suddenly stopped, as though a little bit of wee had come out, and she hurried away onto the bus.

Then Mum gave a tremendous surge, like a tasered eel, and got free of the suited blokes and leapt onto the bus too. She was staggering down the aisle, shouting after Irene's husband to take her with him, and Irene was starting to look really cross. I'd seen her face go that way once before, when someone dropped a hot meat pie in her lap and it wasn't a pretty sight, let me tell you.

The burly blokes were hampered a bit, being so bulky, but they shouldered their way on too, and by the time they reached Mum, the bus was pulling out and Irene's face was all twisted up and inside out looking, and her husband was panicking and trying to get up and sit down at the same time, and I picked up Mum's Primark bag and floated away, as softly and quietly as I do in the dream sequence in the SlumberLoft ad, when my little feathery skis take off from the pillow and I glide away into the dewy forest of that camp fellow's chest hair.

Mum had picked up some lovely bits from Primark, and I was sipping a G and T that evening, taking out the labels and putting in some new ones – just a couple of M&S and a Wallis, I'm not overly fussy – when the news came on the telly. The rumpus on the number nineteen was the headline story. Several people had received crush injuries, two had fallen down the stairs and an undisclosed number had been arrested for indecent exposure. I slipped my needle into the elegant white weave of a Per Una label and stitched on.

Charlotte ate green peppers all day long.

Margaret had this habit of spitting. It began to get on my nerves.

The thing he does with the newspaper.

Camper Van

Josephine Gibson

Charlotte ate green peppers all day long. At least, it seemed all day, because the journey was interminable and when you're stuck in an old VW camper van with people you don't know very well certain things stand out.

Charlotte was hugely pregnant. To be honest, it was distasteful to see her enormous, gross belly, sticking out from a T-shirt that was too small and a pair of hot pants that clung to her hips below a bump covered in blue and red veins. I don't understand why young women think it is attractive to flaunt their fecundity to all and sundry, and I can tell you, there was plenty of it on show as she hauled herself into the van at the start of that journey. Everyone made such a fuss of her and insisted on her sitting at the front, leaving us 'oldies' the bench seats at the back. No thought of how difficult it was for us to unravel our backs at the end of the day.

So Charlotte got in and it wasn't long before she'd stuck her dusty feet, in a pair of flip flops that had seen better days, on the dashboard of the van. Pulling her scrunchie off, she shook her hair and opened the window wide (it squeaked alarmingly, and I worried for a moment that the mechanism might break). No thought for the 'oldies' in the back getting draughty. She opened a large plastic bag and began to eat the peppers as though they were apples, occasionally pulling out the pips and throwing them out of the window. Well, I tried to catch Margaret's eye, but she seemed to be concentrating on holding onto her seatbelt as the van whined around the corners. Perhaps Charlotte saw me, because she suddenly turned and said, "I hope the peppers don't bother you – they're just great for helping me deal with nausea." And then she turned back around without waiting for a reply and patted her stomach smugly.

I was seething – such disrespect. Her boyfriend, sitting next to her, then decided to switch on the radio without consultation and the three in the front (my nephew was driving) all began to sing along with, "We're going to the zoo, zoo, zoo, how about you, you, you." They reminded me of the chimps in the PG Tips adverts, if I'm perfectly honest. I was shuddering and definitely regretted my agreement to be given a lift to the wedding party.

If we'd had my way I would have driven. I love driving. I don't know why Margaret had leapt at the idea of being cooped up in a camper van with three twenty-somethings. I tried to express my opinion, only to be overruled.

"Oh John, it will be fun, it will be a 'road trip' in the proper sense of the word! That VW Camper is so sweet. After all, we're retired, why should it matter if it takes twice as long? And you won't be so tired and grumpy when we get there if you haven't driven."

"Tired and grumpy? I'll probably be more tired and grumpy after sitting in a camper van all day."

"For goodness sake, why not humour me just for once, John?" With a sinking feeling, I recognised the whine as she said my name, a whine that meant I wouldn't be listened to.

"It will do you the world of good to spend some time with the young people," she said. "They're such fun and have so much energy – you never know, some of it might rub off on you."

I didn't know what she was trying to say, but I did begin to feel the stirrings of a little joy as Margaret clutched my hand as we went round another corner. It wasn't long before she began to moan and I had to look out of the window so she couldn't see the corners of my mouth curling into a smile. When she began to retch I almost laughed, but managed to disguise it as a cough and requested my nephew to pull over.

I quite enjoyed the pleasant view of green hills fading into the distance as I took the opportunity to have a stroll in the lay-by while Margaret threw up in the bushes. It was rather disgusting that Charlotte announced that pregnant women need to pee and waved something she called a 'she-wee' at me before she clambered over a fence. I just hoped she didn't try to use it in the van. Really it was quite useful that Margaret had forced a stop; I liked the feeling of the sun on my back and the sound of birds (albeit between the swoosh of articulated lorries as they passed).

All too soon we were back in the van and Margaret looked decidedly peaky. Charlotte proffered her plastic bag, emptying the remaining peppers into her handbag and, I was surprised to note, passed a pack of tissues to Margaret. I hadn't really expected her to be that considerate.

"Right oh," said my nephew, pulling out into the traffic. "We'll have to get a move on now, I hadn't scheduled that stop."

He didn't seem to realise two things. The first was the logical impossibility of getting a move on in an old camper van. The second was that whenever he took a corner as fast as he could, Margaret's car sickness worsened. She tried to be quiet, but after being sick *Margaret had this habit of spitting. It began to get on my nerves.* Both the windows were open now and there was even a suggestion of opening the roof to deal with the smell. I was feeling really chilly but I knew from past experience that my comfort was something people rarely considered. In order to avoid saying something I'd regret later I pulled out my newspaper to distract me.

A few moments later I gave up trying to read. Anymore of that and I'd be as sick as Margaret, to say nothing of the fact the wind blowing through the windows kept slapping the pages in my face. I was starting to feel really angry. This had been a bad idea from start to finish, I'd known all along it was more sensible for me to drive, but as usual my wishes had been overruled. And now here I was, stuck with a sick wife, a pregnant woman gorging on peppers, and a couple of nondescript nincompoops trying to be jovial, in an ancient VW that would probably break down before the end of the day.

"Harrumph!" I couldn't help it, it just slipped out before I could stop it. My nephew glanced at me in the rear view mirror and in order to cover up, I rustled the newspaper on my lap as though I'd read something I didn't like. The next moment the newspaper was flying around the cabin in a strong gust of wind, catching me full on in the face and blowing into the back windows, pages scattering in different directions.

"Stop, stop!" I shouted and I really didn't appreciate the laughter from the front seat.

Later that evening, Margaret had pulled herself together and I did try not to feel too smug (well, to be honest, I relished the moment) when she gratefully accepted the offer of a lift home from my brother and his wife as we sat around the table at the wedding reception.

"I think perhaps John was right," she said, leaning over and patting me on the knee, "we are getting a little old to be gallivanting around the country in a camper van."

I wish I could have recorded the moment – Margaret admitting I was right! But then perhaps it was the effect of the champagne on her empty stomach as she did look a little pink in the cheeks and giggled rather loudly at the best man's speech.

Not as loudly as that wretched girl, Charlotte – who just seemed to be drinking mineral water – standing at the bar with her boyfriend and my nephew. I don't know what they were laughing at but I swear I heard one of them say: *"That thing he does with the newspaper!"*

Peppers, Paps and Old Pals

Kim Kimber

Charlotte ate green peppers all day long... It was the latest in a long list of fad diets that she had been on.

"All the celebrities are doing it," she explained to me and Margaret over lunch. "I've lost half a stone already."

"How long have you been on it?" asked Margaret, through a mouthful of chips. Tall and willowy, even in her late forties, she has always been unsympathetic towards our friend's efforts to lose weight.

"Three, no... today will be the fourth day."

I sipped my vodka and low calorie mixer, my own take on 'cutting down', and regarded the unappetising green vegetables on Charlotte's plate. They had been cooked in olive oil which gave them a slimy sheen. "It's a bit extreme, don't you think? How many do you get through a day?"

"As many as I want. That's the great thing, I've finally found a diet where I can eat as much as I like."

"Just as long as it is green..." Margaret chipped in, "I hope it doesn't turn your face the same colour?"

"As if!" I said, swallowing down a giggle with a sip of my VAT.

"If you eat too many carrots, it can turn you orange, something to do with the carotene. I wondered if was the same for green peppers."

"Don't be ridiculous," said Charlotte, looking hurt. "It's easy for you, Margaret. But I'm tired of being the 'cuddly' one. I want to be able to wear a bikini on our girls' getaway."

Our 'getaway' was a one week stay at a spa hotel in southern Spain. The three of us had been friends since school and the holiday was a treat for our fiftieth birthdays, which fell within a few weeks of one another. We had originally planned to go to the Caribbean and had saved a significant sum. Then the gear box had fallen out of Charlotte's car and Margaret's daughter had decided to get married – rather selfishly I thought – and our 'holiday pot' had dwindled.

"I just don't know how you can bear to eat so many green peppers, it's not even like they taste good."

"I don't care, if it works," Charlotte said.

I had some sympathy for her. I would do practically anything to lose a stone – except maybe eat nothing but green peppers all day.

"Let me try a bit," said Margaret, spearing a piece of green vegetable with her fork and popping it into her mouth.

"That... is... disgusting," she said, gagging theatrically before ejecting the pepper forcibly from her mouth, peppering Charlotte and me with specks of green.

"Ugh!" said Charlotte, wiping a line of green freckles from her face with a napkin.

Margaret had this habit of spitting... out her food when she didn't like something.

Over the years, *it had begun to get on my nerves* and I wondered whether I could tolerate the company of my friends for a whole week.

"Was that really necessary?" said Charlotte in disgust.

"Sorry, couldn't help it," Margaret replied, taking a huge swig of gin and tonic. "I hope you're not going to be on this stupid diet when we're on holiday."

"No, Wayne doesn't like it when I'm picky with my food. He's got such a big appetite, he'll want to tuck into platefuls of steaming paella."

"Wayne!" Margaret and I shouted in unison. "What's he got to do with it?"

Charlotte coloured and looked guilty, "Well... he didn't want us to be parted, so..."

"So what?" Margaret asked. "Please tell me that you didn't..."

Charlotte nodded.

"It's not going to be much of a girls' getaway with Wayne in tow," Margaret pointed out.

"He won't be any trouble, you'll hardly notice he's there. In fact it works out better because now you two can have one room and I can share the other with Wayne."

"Terrific!" sighed Margaret.

Wayne was Charlotte's latest man-friend. Like her diets, there had been a lot of them in recent years. Several years her junior, Wayne was even less desirable in my opinion than Charlotte's past boyfriends. I had only met him once but he had prattled on endlessly about the best waxing products for chest hair and how much you should pay for a spray tan – as if I would know?

"It's supposed to be a treat for the three of us, we're going to a spa. What's Wayne going to do while we get our toxins purged in a hot mud body wrap?" asked Margaret.

I thought back to my first meeting with Wayne and could guess the answer.

"You don't like him do you?" Charlotte asked looking at me.

"Yes, no… I don't know. He just seemed a bit…"

"A bit what?"

"Self-obsessed…"

"Vain and irritating!" added Margaret, signalling to the waiter for another G and T. "It's *the thing he does with the newspaper.*"

"What newspaper? What thing?"

"You know, hides behind it every five minutes, as if he's being followed."

"He's not wanted by the police is he?" Margaret asked.

Charlotte giggled, "No, it's not that. It's in case he gets spotted by the paps."

"The what?" I asked blankly.

"Paparazzi! Wayne is an actor, he's appeared in *EastEnders*. He might get snapped by the press and then our photos would be all over the papers."

"Well, at least that explains the need for sunglasses in the middle of winter," quipped Margaret. "But I don't recall having seen him in *EastEnders* and I never miss an episode."

"No, well, maybe it hasn't aired yet. But he's been in lots of other things."

"You could be dating Johnny Depp for all I care, he can't come on our holiday."

"But..."

"Speaking of whom, look, over there," I said, grabbing Charlotte's arm. "Isn't that your Wayne peeking out from behind the *Daily Mirror*?"

It was Wayne. This time the newspaper served another purpose, to hide the fact that he was draped all over another girl.

"That bitch! I hate her!" sobbed Charlotte. "She's so... so..."

"Common," suggested Margaret.

"THIN!"

Charlotte gestured to the waiter. "Could I have a plate of chips please, oh and a VAT; best make it a large one."

"I'll show him," said Charlotte, heading towards Wayne with the redundant dish of green peppers.

Wayne looked stunned as Charlotte approached and tipped the lot over his head. Green slime dripped down his designer sunglasses and onto his chin. As he whipped them off to wipe his face, there was an explosion of lights as several photographers descended on his table.

"I guess he must be famous after all," I said laughing. "Sorry, Charlotte."

"I hope this means the holiday is back on," added Margaret.

"Definitely. I've had more than enough of men."

Margaret and I ordered more drinks and when they arrived we raised our glasses.

"To Spain!"

"And friendship," Charlotte added, "my men, like diets, don't last for long, but I know that whatever happens I can always depend on my two best pals."

Carnage in the Kitchen

Barbara Sleap

Charlotte was very unhappy with the hotel in Cyprus. The newspaper article she had with her had given the food a five star rating but *Charlotte ate green peppers all day*, well that's what it felt like. And not just green; red, orange and yellow, too. Peppers stuffed with rice, peppers stuffed with cous cous and, at breakfast this morning, one stuffed with egg and cheese. It was beginning to affect her digestive system; she had a lot of wind which was becoming an embarrassment and she still had another two weeks before going home. What's more her friend, *Margaret, had developed a habit of spitting. It began to get on Charlotte's nerves*, but Margaret said Charlotte wouldn't have such a bad stomach if she spat out those little white seeds.

Charlotte felt she had to do something drastic. She had complained to the manager but he said the chef had a free rein in the kitchen and there had been a glut of peppers this year.

The kitchen was a 'no go' area to guests but Charlotte and Margaret had been watching and knew that it was always empty around four in the afternoon when everyone was snoozing. So at 4.00 p.m. they stole furtively through the forbidden door. They were surprised how clean and tidy it all was with gleaming stainless steel units and every utensil you could think of, including two mean looking meat axes, which they took from the rack. They both crept stealthily round the units and suddenly Margaret gasped.

"There they are."

Sure enough four large crates were stacked up in a corner and through the bars Charlotte could see the offending vegetables. They set to and began hacking into the top crate. Coloured juices spattered their clothes and their skin. Margaret had an almost evil grin as her arms thrashed down onto the now mushy mess. They were about to start on the next crate when a loud voice pierced through the room.

"What you do, what you do, uh?"

Charlotte stared at the bulging-eyed chef and shouted, "Peppers, peppers, peppers, we are all sick of them, can't you cook anything else?"

With that she pulled the newspaper from her beach bag and stabbed at the article with a wet green finger.

"Call this five star food…"

But before she could say another word the red faced chef snarled and snatched the newspaper from Charlotte's sticky hand; pushing her aside he rolled it into a fat tube. At this point Charlotte dropped her knife and tried to run but in doing so she slipped on the slimy floor where she cowered down in fright. Margaret stood rooted to the floor. Well, *the things he did with that newspaper!*

Charlotte and Margaret didn't go to the hotel restaurant that night but had dinner at the 'Mighty Meaty Kebab Hut' in town, with plenty of onion – but not a single pepper!

After only two months, Helen decided to become an exotic dancer.

She started picking up a lot of bad habits.

The day Lillian learned to drive.

Bernard!

Trisha Todd

After only two months Helen decided to become an exotic dancer, anything would be better than sitting across the desk from Bernard five days a week. She felt sure that, as the newbie, she'd been given the worst seat in the office.

Glancing over the top of her computer at Bernard, she remembered the embarrassment of her first day, when she was sure she had stepped in something on her way in to the office. It took her a couple of hours to realise the smell was rolling across from Bernard's desk like a toxic cloud. She swore she could discern a greenish tinge to the air too!

Bernard was currently eating a ham salad sandwich, and Helen found it hideously compelling viewing – was the lettuce going to stay between the curled white slices or, more likely, freefall down his tie to land in the gap between his shirt buttons, covering his hairy, white belly which was normally on view? He looked over at her and smiled; a piece of tomato skin adorned his front teeth.

Helen shuddered and endeavoured to look busy. In her peripheral vision she could see Bernard lick his hand and smooth it over his lank, greying hair. He finished his sandwich and belched loudly, tittering as he excused himself to any within hearing distance. Helen stood up and dashed for the kitchen; a cup of tea would calm her nerves.

Maisie already had the kettle on, and she set another cup out on the counter for Helen. "How are you doing?" she asked.

"Oh, the job is fine, it's just Bernard. I don't think I can take much more," Helen groaned. "It's not only that his hygiene leaves something to be desired, or the burping whenever he eats anything, it's just I've noticed *I'm starting to pick up his bad habits* – the other day I nearly licked my hand to smooth down my fringe!" She began to titter, then looked at Maisie, aghast. "Oh my G…od," she stuttered. "I'm turning into Bernard!"

That evening, she drove to her parents' house to collect her younger sister, Lillian. "Come on Lil," Helen called. *"Today is the day you learn to drive."* She flapped the magnetic 'L' plates at Lillian as she came down the stairs.

After a jumpy start, Lillian gained reasonable control of Helen's Mini and drove, albeit slowly, along the High Street. At that hour, the shops were closed and shuttered, and just a couple of cars shared the road with them. "Turn left here, Lil," Helen instructed. "We'll try a three-point turn." As Lillian turned into the side street, an advertising hoarding caught Helen's eye. It was for a recently opened nightclub – 'Dancers Wanted'. *Hmmm,* she thought, remembering her half-serious decision at work that morning.

By the time Saturday afternoon arrived, Helen had bravely decided to try out at the nightclub. Feeling slightly self-conscious in high heels, sequinned T-shirt and shorts, she gyrated around the pole. "Okay, that's enough," the manager said. "You can come back tonight at nine and we'll see how you get on." He handed her a bag. "Wear this."

Nine o'clock saw Helen garbed in the short, red dress she'd been given. She paced the floor of the changing room while one of the other dancers was on stage, then went to the door and peered around the edge. She scanned the darkened room, noting that the club was filling up fast. The music was pulsing, lights flashing. Helen did a double take – had she seen someone familiar? She waited for the light to sweep across the section in front of the dance floor, and spotted – Bernard!

Helen couldn't change into her own clothes quick enough, mumbling her apologies as she ran outside. "I think I'll just request a transfer on Monday," she chuckled to herself.

Shake, Rattle and Run

Barbara Sleap

Helen loved to dance, she had been to many different classes and, since childhood, had tried ballet, tap, salsa, jazz and jive but she had never tried belly dancing. She, therefore, was intrigued when she saw an advert for 'Shakira's Belly Dance Course'. So, with her friend, Lillian, she enrolled for the twice-weekly sessions.

At first, Helen found it difficult to separate her belly area from the rest of her body but she loved the music and the movements and persevered. She purchased an exotic Middle Eastern-style costume, complete with tiny bells and tassels. Helen liked the feel of the silky shimmering skirt as she moved within it and the soft golden slippers with a pom pom on the front. *After only two months, Helen had decided she wanted to be an exotic dancer*. Lillian did not complete the course, she said it was embarrassing for a middle-aged woman to carry on in that way and, anyway, she wanted to concentrate on her driving lessons.

Helen booked extra lessons with Shakira (whose real name was Sharon) and practiced whenever possible. Shakira showed her how to make up her eyes to look dark and seductive. Helen wiggled and sashayed wherever she happened to be; at the bus stop, in the supermarket and at work. The men in the estate agency where she was an administrative assistant shyly lowered their eyes when she shimmied up to them provocatively with her latest typed report. After some months Helen felt proficient enough to advertise herself as 'Jasmina, Exotic Dancer – available for short performances at parties, stag nights and cabarets'.

It wasn't long before Helen had several bookings and the first was at a small business convention in a local hotel. The group of businessmen had been wined and dined before Jasmina's act. She stood in the ladies' toilets waiting for her call and was so nervous that her red tassels and silver bells were damp with perspiration. But after her solo performance she lured some of the men onto the floor; they took it all in good part and tried to copy her movements, even though they looked foolish as their oversized bellies wobbled to the music. It had been a success, she had enjoyed herself and been paid a fair sum too.

Full of confidence, 'Jasmina' arrived at her next booking, a stag party being held in a small room at the back of a local pub and it was here that *she started picking up a lot of bad habits*. The young men were a bit loud and also quite drunk. This unnerved Helen at first but she was soon spinning around to their raucous calls and whistling. They bought her a few drinks and soon she was belly dancing, not just on the floor, but on their laps, or leaning over them eyeing them sexily from behind her golden veil. Towards the end of the evening one of the men, Steve, got a bit carried away and pulled her on to the floor. He was a great mover and together they performed an exotic routine to the cheers of the rest of the group who by this time were all very drunk. This led to rather more than Helen expected as they both ended up in her flat and Steve didn't leave until the early hours next morning.

Helen decided that she wouldn't take on any more stag bookings after that and vowed not to accept alcohol during future performances.

***

A few weeks later, Helen arrived at the door of her third engagement that night; a party given by a woman named Tania for her husband's thirtieth birthday. Jasmina was to be part of the surprise. This was also the day that *Lillian had finally learned to drive.* She had passed her test only the day before and for her first outing had offered to drive Helen to the venue in her mum's car. Afterwards, they were planning to go to a club together to celebrate.

Tania opened the front door, putting her fingers to her lips as she took Jasmina's CD out of her hands. She then disappeared, leaving Helen conspicuously uncomfortable in the hallway where she was eyed curiously by other guests. It was a noisy affair and Helen felt uneasy. Suddenly, her Egyptian music rang out and a familiar, dark curly head appeared round the doorway.

Helen's hand flew to her mouth and Steve gasped and nearly choked on his beer. Tania chose this moment to follow him out grinning widely. She took one look at Jasmina and her husband and her grin gradually faded into a snarl. Before Tania could turn back to face Steve, Helen grabbed her bag and fled through the still open front door, ignoring Tania's angry shouts from behind. She leapt into the car telling a perplexed, wide-eyed Lillian to, "Just drive."

As they drove away, Lillian asked, "Jasmina wasn't a success tonight then?"

To which Helen replied, "I'm thinking of taking up Zumba!"

Westchurch Surprise

Sue Duggans

Jeannie had worked as a call centre operative for the past three years – a job, she had decided in the first month, she wouldn't wish on her worst enemy. Relentless tedium! The highlight of her day was when the buzzer went at ten-thirty, announcing tea break for Team A. Fifteen minutes and no more or else the wrath of the menacing section supervisor Denise, known as 'Denis', would fall on them!

Then one day, the boredom was interrupted briefly by an unexpected 'pop-up' which caught Jeannie's eye and imagination.

'Unleash the Goddess Within!'

The headline beckoned and Jeannie read on. An exciting new dance class, promising to improve fitness and flexibility, enhance weight loss and offer a new lease of life, was opening just a short bus ride from her studio flat in Shoreditch. Just what she needed to lift her out of the rut in which she was jammed and brighten up her less than sparkling social life. She scribbled the details on a Post-it note and returned to her target list. Only another four hours and twenty-three minutes of her shift remaining.

Jeannie was usually confident but, as she entered the basement studio for her first dance class, butterflies fluttered relentlessly in her stomach. However, she was afforded a warm welcome by Tania, the sylph-like dance teacher, clad in shocking-pink.

The group of seven limbered up to strains of 'Do Ya Think I'm Sexy?' and danced their way through a variety of increasingly complicated routines. Glistening with perspiration Jeannie had really got into her stride when the session concluded to the rhythm of 'Hit Me Baby One More Time'.

"See you next week," Jeannie called over her shoulder to Tania and the other girls as she left in time to catch the nine fifty-two back to her flat. She was already looking forward to the next class with an intangible excitement.

Over the next few weeks Tania taught the group well and took them through 'Ten Easy Steps to Becoming an Exotic Dancer':

- Realise that this is a job, not a lifestyle.
- Get kitted out – four inch heels and a selection of coordinated outfits.
- Wax from the neck downwards, never shave.
- Think up a suitable stage name.
- Be mentally strong.
- Keep safe.

The list went on and, for Jeannie, a storm of anticipation and excitement was brewing.

"Keep your chin up, look confident, and go for it, girls!" was Tania's mantra. It was clear that she made a very decent living from teaching and performing at her club and she appeared to want the same for her 'girls'.

After only two months, Jeannie decided to become an exotic dancer full time and eagerly handed in her notice at the call centre. Initially, she worked at Tania's club in Soho. Work started at eight in the evening and concluded at around 3.00 a.m. Tania insisted that her dancers went home in a cab although, sometimes, the wait meant that Jeannie didn't slip back into the security and comfort of her flat until after four in the morning when the city was beginning to come back to life. *It wasn't long before she started picking up an assortment of bad habits* and, for the first time, questioned whether her usually good judgement had become clouded.

Then, out of the blue, a potential opportunity came her way. Early one Tuesday evening, before setting off for the club, Jeannie's mobile rang. A quick check revealed that the caller was unknown to her.

"Hi, Jeannie. My name is Rosalie and I'm the secretary of the Women's Institute in Westchurch. It's our group's first birthday in April and Sue Jones from the call centre said you might be able to provide entertainment for our celebration."

The line went horribly quiet as Jeannie tried to take in what Rosalie had just said. Her first solo engagement! Would she be able to go through with it?

'Unleash the Goddess Within!' The headline that had started it all popped up in her head. With an imperceptible tremor in her voice, Jeannie replied with feigned confidence, "Yep, sounds good to me. I'll need to check dates and get back to you. Can you let me have your name and number?"

Westchurch was on the outskirts of a Sussex seaside town. Jeannie had been there only once, some years ago, to visit her Uncle William, who had moved with his wife, Ann, and their daughter Claire to take up a new job at the council offices. Since then, a family argument led to an unresolved rift. It happened at a Christmas family gathering when Jeannie's dad, disapproving of Claire's short skirt and heavy make-up and being 'worse the wear' for drink, described her as a tart! William hit the roof, the two men never spoke again and family gatherings come to an end.

Jeannie travelled down during the afternoon with her good friend, Lillian. They'd hired a Renault Clio which had to be back by ten the next morning. *It was the day Lillian learned to drive* without 'L' plates, having passed her test that very morning, and she was desperate to get behind the wheel. Jeannie was nervous enough and wouldn't hear of it! She had taken Lillian out for a driving lesson on two occasions. The second was even more terrifying than the first! Lillian loved putting her foot down and thought speed limits were an irrelevance. The friends arrived late in the afternoon and took the opportunity to stroll on the seafront and enjoy the energising sea breeze.

They arrived at the venue with plenty of time for Jeannie to prepare. Rosalie, an efficient-looking woman in her early fifties, met them at the door and showed them into a small room containing a number of red plastic chairs, low tables and, mercifully, a full-length mirror on the wall.

Jeannie slipped into the scarlet, halter-neck dress which she'd chosen for the event. It was, she thought, modest enough for the occasion. Her nails were painted in matching scarlet and her lipstick coordinated perfectly. She completed her outfit with expensive perfume, black shoes (four inch heels) and a little black hat tilted precariously on the top of her head. A quick peek in the mirror confirmed that she'd do. Lillian gave her a reassuring hug and a peck on the cheek. She slipped from the holding room and into the hall whilst Jeannie, mouth dry, waited for Rosalie.

In no time, Jeannie found herself stepping into the hall to the subdued strains of 'Do Ya Think I'm Sexy?'. Forty or so women sat politely in small groups around tables. A 'Happy First Birthday' banner hung at the front of the hall and each table was decked with a small posy of flowers. Jeannie was led to the front to be introduced to the guests of honour – his Worshipful the Mayor and his wife, the Lady Mayoress. Jeannie stopped, her face turning as scarlet as her dress.

The Mayor rose to his feet and stepped towards her, a twinkle in his eye.

"Uncle Bill, Aunty Ann," Jeannie spoke softly. "What an unexpected pleasure."

As he drew his niece towards him and kissed her fondly, the Mayor whispered in her ear, "Your grandmother would turn in her grave."

Themed poems

Places

The Perfect Day

Barbara Sleap

I've seen many places, travelled far and wide,
Of life in the world I've seen many a side,
So I have imagined one perfect day,
From the wondrous sights I've seen on my way.

I'll wake up in Luxor and listen a while
To the Imam's call echoing across the Nile.
A felucca to Karnak amid ancient columns
These pillars have seen many golden suns.

A flight on to Jordan, to Petra where it's said
That the old city at dawn glows a true rose red.
Sit in a tent at Wadi Rum for tea,
Then a cool reviving float in the salty Dead Sea.

I'll have lunch in Venice on St Mark's Square
Watch the bustling crowd without a care.
Take a gondola ride, with maybe a song
The water swirling gently as we drift along.

This time travel tour maybe a long haul
As I reach Beijing and the majestic Great Wall,
The Forbidden City has secrets to behold
Temples, pagodas and Buddhas of gold.

It's Vegas for dinner at the Hotel New York
A rollercoaster ride here leaves no time to talk.
A ten dollar flutter then to Gracelands I'll go
To remember 'The King'; he lives on I know.

The last leg of my day, it's been a long one,
Is to visit Grand Canyon for the setting of the sun
The colours on the rocks, such an awesome sight
And I linger a while as day turns to night.

I've enjoyed my memories on this imaginary jaunt
Just a few of the places I've been able to haunt.
Without travel my life would have been incomplete
There's more places to see 'cos I've got itchy feet.

Blue Kite in a Tree

Josephine Gibson

A remnant of summer
Caught
In a wind wizened tree.

A reminder
Of childhood shrieks
Of small brown hands
And a trusting body
Now grown beyond my reach.

Bold indigo
And cotton candy stripes
Against the eggshell sky.

Like the kite
You soar
No thought for
Your earthbound anchor
Now you are free.

(Thorpe Bay, Essex, September 2014)

The Sea and Southend Pier

Lois Maulkin

Managing to be both dirty
And clean at the same time,
Salt grey gravy laps the pier legs.

Trains half-hour the mile and a third into bites.
Below, through clanking, planky gaps,
Whelks lurk murkily in choppy rubble.

Fishermen trudge, buskers breathe the briny,
Chip fat, bladderwrack, Chanel No°5.
Beige scum sucks the pilings.

Unseen by captains, torched by faglight,
Crunched and ground to powder,
The pier withstands, year on year.

Holding itself up from the pull down
Into the queasy, uneasy movement.
Rippled seabed, chunks of pebble-dash.

Absurdly, diamondly, spankingly alive
In the bleach and twinkle sunshine,
Remorseless waves, just playing,

Slap, slap, slap, slap, smack you away.
As the seagulls chew the audible bits of sky,
And your barnacley cellulite clings.

About the Authors

Sue Duggans

Sue has lived in the Southend area for most of her life. During her time at Teacher Training College in London in the early '70s, she studied English and had many creative writing opportunities.

Having joined the WoSWI writing group, the pleasure and stimulation of writing were reawakened for her. The monthly meetings provide shared writing opportunities, fun and laughter!

Josephine Gibson

Josephine spent her childhood living at the edge of Surrey woodlands, and her teenage years living in a remote location on Dartmoor. Subsequently, she has lived in the Cotswolds, the Midlands and Essex.

Constant moving and the experience of solitude in vast expanses of moorland has made her somewhat of an outside observer who is happy alone but also loves being with people and listening to their experiences. Reading and learning new ideas are important to her, as is walking by the Thames Estuary and watching its ever changing light. She is married with three grown up children.

Kim Kimber

Kim is an Advanced Professional Member of the Society for Editors and Proofreaders (SfEP) and has helped many first time authors on the road to publication. In the past, Kim has had several articles published in magazines and newspapers and currently compiles quiz questions on popular culture.

Kim became a member of WoSWI in 2011 and formed the writing group shortly afterwards. She is proud of the group's achievements which include the publication of its first anthology *Write on the Coast* in 2013. She hopes that this second book, *Ten Minute Tales*, will be as well received as the first.

Lois Maulkin

Still living in a small, damp house, still (thank the Lord) mother to four, and still not knowing what I'm going to do when I grow up, very little has changed since my biographical notes in *Write on the Coast*, except that I now have a new cat, which smells quite a bit less than the old one.

Barbara Sleap

I may be the oldest member of the group but, at 68, I am active and young at heart. I retired from my job as a travel consultant aged 60 and thoroughly enjoy spending time with my family and friends. I am never bored, especially with five grandchildren to keep me busy. I enjoy aqua aerobics, holidaying whenever possible and, as an avid reader, I belong to two book groups.

I joined WoSWI three years ago to spend time with like-minded ladies. I was eager to join the writing group as I have always been a bit of a scribbler. The group, for me, has been such an enlightening experience and, with Kim's expert guidance, my writing has become more focused. Our meetings are interesting, often hilarious, and always challenging. I love listening to the different styles and thoughts of my fellow members and look forward to many more projects.

Trisha Todd

I live in Prittlewell, Southend-on-Sea, work in Rochford and spend my time reading, writing, gardening, learning Spanish and generally anything else I can find to get me out of doing the housework. I share my life with my lovely expanding family and our slightly mad dog.

Westcliff-on-Sea Women's Institute

WESTCLIFF-ON-SEA WOMEN'S INSTITUTE

(Registered Charity No. XT 36711)

From hoteliers to decorators, teachers to full-time mums, there isn't a typical member of Westcliff-on-Sea Women's Institute (WoSWI). We come from all walks of life, and cover all age ranges.

Based in Westcliff-on-Sea, in Essex, what we do have in common is a dedication to having fun, enjoying the company of interesting women, supporting and getting involved with our community, broadening our horizons and learning new skills, as well as occasionally indulging in the odd tipple!

Our interests include crafts (it is the WI!), culture, education and social activities. Since our first meeting in September 2009, hundreds of women have come along to see what WoSWI is all about. Many have joined our sub-groups from cycling and walking to reading and writing, where they have made friends and taken up new hobbies.

Each year, WoSWI members vote on a local charity to support and raise money for. This year we have chosen The South Essex Branch of the Motor Neurone Disease Association and we hope to match the success of previous years in raising significant sums for our chosen charity.

If you would like to find out more about WoSWI or are interested in joining us, visit our website below.

www.westcliffwi.co.uk

The South Essex Branch of the Motor Neurone Disease Association

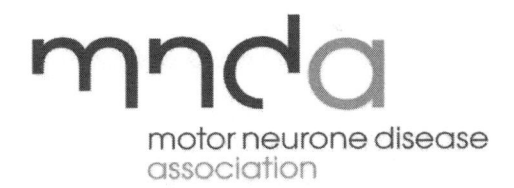

mnda
motor neurone disease
association

(Registered Charity No. 294354)

Motor neurone disease (MND) is a progressive disease that attacks the motor neurones, or nerves, in the brain and spinal cord. Degeneration of the motor neurones leads to weakness and wasting of muscles, causing increasing loss of mobility in the limbs, and difficulties with speech, swallowing and breathing.

The effects of MND can vary enormously from person to person, from the presenting of symptoms, and the rate and pattern of the disease progression, to the length of survival time after diagnosis.

The South Essex Branch of the Motor Neurone Disease Association has the sole aim of serving all those in the area who are affected by this disease. This includes people with MND, their carers, family and friends; in fact anyone who has been touched in some way by the disease.

They liaise with health and social care professionals such as speech therapists, occupational therapists and the medical profession, attending the monthly multiple disciplinary meetings at both Southend and Basildon Hospitals.

The Branch holds regular support meetings for people living with MND and their carers. These provide an opportunity to meet with other people living with the disease, and a chance to share experiences and ideas.

The South Essex Branch is run entirely by volunteers, many of whom have personal experience of the disease.

There is currently no cure for MND.

www.mndsouthessex.org